Annie True and Brave

Jody Day

This is a work of fiction. Names, characters, places, and incidents either are the product of the author's imagination or are used fictitiously, and any resemblance to actual persons living or dead, business establishments, events, or locales, is entirely coincidental.

Cover Art by *Nicola Martinez*
Harbourlight Books, a division of Pelican Ventures, LLC
www.pelicanbookgroup.com PO Box 1738 *Aztec, NM * 87410
Harbourlight Books sail and mast logo is a trademark of Pelican Ventures, LLC

Publishing History: First Harbourlight Edition, 2025
Paperback Edition ISBN 978-1-5223-0535-4
Electronic Edition ISBN 978-1-5223-0533-0
Published in the United States of America

Dedication

Father God, I'm forever grateful. For Annie Riggs, a true pioneer who modeled strength, strong values and faith to a fledgling town in the wild West. Thank you Andi Martin for first hiring me to work at the Fort years ago. Your enthusiasm for Fort Stockton's history caught fire in me and well, here we are. Thank you Elva Valadez, Director of the Fort Stockton Public Library and former president and treasurer of the Fort Stockton Historical Society, and Melba Montoya, former director of the Historic Fort and the Annie Riggs Memorial Museum, for all your help and support throughout the years I was learning about Annie. Critique Cafe, Fort Stockton Area Writers Group, thanks once again for your excellent support, suggestions, and encouragement. As always, thank you to my husband Randy and my family for always supporting me.

What People are Saying

Annie True and Brave is an awe inspiring novel filled with historical figures and how their lives played a part in settling Fort Stockton. ~ Frances Gomez Armstrong.

Annie True and Brave is a wild ride. It paints a very clear and beautiful picture of the West Texas atmosphere and what life was like for the people of the time. In this book we get to experience Annie's life, which was harrowing, emotional, tragic, exciting, and full of surprises. Such an interesting and inspiring read! ~ Sarah Hamilton

Chapter 1

April 1901

The only thing standing between Annie Riggs's future, freedom, and most dire, her safety, was Barney Riggs. He stood before her red-faced, set-jawed, and gripping a can of coal oil. He stared her down, and Annie sensed he considered his next move. Whatever he decided could mean harm for Annie and her children. His whiskey-fueled rage always flashed like a desert brush fire, destroying everything in its path until it hit dirt, where there was nothing left to burn. His usual subsequent repentance in the proverbial dust and ashes, and often on his knees, would not work this time, *if* she lived through this latest aggression. She steeled herself, the coal oil fumes bringing on dizziness.

Only ten years old, Junior huddled in the corner with his younger siblings. Errol, Mavis, and baby Gene clutched at his shirt and sobbed.

"Papa, please," Junior cried.

Barney jerked his head toward his son, and Annie's heart lurched.

Junior fished in his pants pocket and pulled out a rock. His knuckles went white as he gripped the rock in his fist. "Please, Pa, don't."

Barney took a step toward his children, and Junior took a step toward his father.

Errol picked up baby Gene and grabbed Mavis' hand. Their cries tore at Annie.

Junior held the rock up as if to throw it.

Barney's jaw went slack, and his blue eyes glazed over. Was he having a stroke? He dropped the coal oil can and the putrid liquid streamed a path across the cabin floor. He turned toward the bedroom door. Giving up? Or reaching for his rifle that leaned against the wall?

She couldn't risk it. As soon as he was fully turned away, she took the most important deep breath of her life and shouted, "Run!"

~*~

The next day...

Annie made up her mind. She tried to focus on Doña Piña's small spare room. The old sutlery with its thick, adobe walls kept the room cool, and the crazy quilt that hung on the window shielded Annie from the morning sun. She tried to focus on the way the feather mattress and heavy quilts cocooned her. Safe for the moment, she should have been able to sleep, but even after bathing, coal oil from her hair stung her nose and made her eyes water.

The scratches on her legs throbbed, so she couldn't block out the flight through the desert the night before. There hadn't been time to grab a shawl or wrap, or anything to start a fire. She and the children spent the night huddled against a pile of rocks. The little ones, wrapped up in her skirts, jolted awake with the whine and bark of the coyotes. Annie shushed them back to sleep, stroking their damp foreheads. She thought about how Pa would once more tell her, "I told you not to marry him."

As a child, she'd loved the desert night song, the rhythm of the crickets, and the howl of coyotes and wolves. Pa had moved them to Fort Stockton when she was only eight. They'd slept in a tent then. She'd lie awake and listen to the constant roar of the wind. It never frightened her.

But last night, the longest night of her life, the fear had constricted her throat. The darkness had hidden her silent grief from the children. She'd wept for the dreams broken once more. By the time the sun peeped over the eastern mesa, she'd set her mind on what would come next.

Never again. Her heart broke once more as she recalled how Junior had held up a rock in threat to his father, tears streaming down his face. Annie Riggs would never run again. She'd lifted her head and walked straight as a rod out of the desert the next morning.

They'd stumbled into town at dawn. Annie hadn't seen any flames in the darkness, so her house, or rather, Barney's house, must still be standing. What did it matter? He'd destroyed most of the furniture anyway. Whatever remained would reek of coal oil. She'd never step foot inside that house again. His horse was tied to the rail as they passed the saloon. Had Barney slept it off in the back room?

The children had clung to her skirts and whimpered when they saw their father's horse. She had no fear of confronting him. He knew her well enough to know that what he'd done last night would end it, once and for all. She'd knocked on Doña Matilde Piña's door.

The woman took one look at the bedraggled troop and spun into action. She put the kettle on, and then fed the children and put them to bed. She heated more water for a bath and gave Annie some privacy. Doña Matilde came in later and gathered buckets. She'd rinsed Annie's hair three times, but the scent of coal oil lingered.

"*Pobre cosa, mija,* you must sleep," the old woman said as she lay a fresh nightgown on the chair beside the tub. "No work today. No, you sleep. I will speak to Mr. Kettler." She clucked more endearments in broken English and crossed herself as she tucked Annie in like a child.

Sleep. If only she could. In a few hours she would send for fresh clothes from the house so she could see her father this afternoon. Surely his position as Pecos County Judge could expedite things. She counted her assets for a fresh start – her faith, good, strong children, and a job at the Kettler Hotel. She let that thought comfort her. But despite her resolve, she pulled the spare pillow into her arms and wept.

~*~

A Year Later ~ April 8, 1902

Annie pounded the dough into shape. If she didn't stop manhandling it, the biscuits would be hard as rocks. She punched her fist into the wooden bowl one more time and then watched the imprint of her knuckles spread and disappear. She lifted the dough and threw it down on the floured kitchen table. A puff of flour misted the air as she began to roll it out.

"Something wrong, Mrs. Riggs?" Abel Martin stood in the kitchen door, both arms loaded with packages from Kettler's store. He blew blond bangs out of his face.

"Just put the packages on the end of the table there." How had she not heard him come in?

Abel unloaded the groceries on the end of the table. "Mr. Riggs is kicking up a ruckus at the saloon. Heard him hollerin' as I passed."

She slammed the rolling pin down on the table. "Hasn't your mama taught you to mind your own business?"

The blood drained from Abel's ruddy face. He blew his bangs up again, revealing wide, frightened blue eyes. He headed for the door.

What's the matter with me? "Wait, Abel." She stepped across the kitchen and took two cookies from the glass jar by the stove.

Abel stood by the door, frozen.

Annie walked over to him and picked up one stiff arm, opened his fingers and placed the cookies in his palm. She then took a penny from her apron and tucked it in his tattered shirt pocket. She grasped both his shoulders and looked into his eyes. "You stay away from that saloon, you hear me?"

He relaxed and took a bite of cookie. "Yes, ma'am. You and Mama agree on that."

"You listen to your mama, then." Annie turned the boy around and nudged him toward the door. If Susanna Martin didn't do it soon, Annie might as well tie that boy to a chair and cut off those long blond curls. At thirteen, he was pretty nearly a man. Susanna seemed to fall ill often these days. Annie worried a bit about her having a new baby in such a frail condition, and her husband recently cold in the grave. Maybe she just didn't have time or energy to worry over Abel's hair. The poor boy had been run ragged since his pa died.

She followed him to the front door and closed it behind him, glancing through the lace door curtain at the saloon across the street. Just a few horses tied to the rail, but not Barney's. But then, he hadn't been getting around very well lately.

He used a cane the last time she'd seen him. Who would take care of him if his health declined? He'd taken that out of her hands. Some, especially his best friend, Charlie Simmons, said she'd left him all alone. It's not as if she wanted to divorce him, but a woman's mind, body, and heart, could only take so much. He'd taken all but her spirit, and that nearly broken.

He made it hard for her to enjoy her freedom. He wouldn't leave things alone. Why couldn't he just agree to the terms and let them all get on with their lives? Eleven children between them, and her heart still connected to his. Would it ever be over?

The clock on the foyer wall showed nearly noon. Her steps turned toward the kitchen. Time to finish cutting those biscuits and get lunch ready for the school children. Thank heaven the ranchers paid her to feed their children during the week. Every little bit of extra work she could get added to her salary as manager of the Kettler Hotel. She couldn't get a dime from Barney until he agreed to the financial terms of their divorce.

"Annie!"

Oh, no, that sounds like Barney. What now?

"Annie girl, come and look!"

She made her way back to the front and stepped out the door.

Barney sat on his buckboard, reins in hand. He kept yelling for her.

Of all things! A rotting bovine carcass sprawled in the wagon, flies buzzing around.

"What in the world are you doing, Barney Riggs?" The smell from the carcass turned her stomach.

"Look, Annie girl, I finally got someone to ride with me!"

The crowd that had gathered outside the Grey Mule Saloon across the street snickered and pointed.

Annie turned, flew back into the hotel, and slammed the door. This was her punishment for refusing to go for a ride with him to discuss a reconciliation. His repeated requests wore her down, but her mind was made up. Never again. She peeked out the curtains once again.

He drove down the road toward Rooney Park. He talked to himself, spewing expletives no doubt.

Annie sighed and willed her tears to stay at bay. *I've got work to do.* She returned to the kitchen and looked out the window.

Callie Smith sat in the backyard; rough, black hands folded in her lap. Thin and gaunt, Callie waited for Monday's laundry, her mahogany eyes staring toward the north, the direction her Lucius rode the last time she saw him. She'd been a laundress for the Fort when she and Lucius had "jumped the broom" on the Fort grounds. Annie attended the ceremony, to the shocked sentiment of the officers' wives. When the Fort disbanded and prepared to ride out, Callie was pregnant and nearing her time. Lucius promised to come for her. He never did. Annie could sometimes get Callie to come into the hotel for a cup of tea, but rarely.

Annie continued to cut the dough and put the rounds in the oven, then set to slicing ham. Her thoughts went to poor Beau. Her oldest daughter, Maddie, had a real gem of a husband in Beau Chadwick. He'd taken over as executor of the divorce settlement, and Barney was giving him a murderous time. Beau had even petitioned the court to be relieved. Annie didn't blame him, but what would she do without help? Just the day before Beau had tried to talk to Barney, but was rewarded with several blows of his cane. She'd just have to pray harder for a resolution to the situation and not rant at innocent errand boys.

The bell on the front door dinged, and she

expected to hear the shuffling of children's feet, and the scraping of chairs at the dining room table. She didn't hear anything, but maybe it was a guest wanting a bed. She walked through the kitchen and dining room to the front foyer, brushing flour from her hands against her apron. "Maddie!" Annie called to her daughter who stood leaning on the counter, her hat disheveled. Maddie's hand clutched at her waist, and she gasped for breath.

"What's the matter?" Annie put her arm around Maddie, led her to the dining room table, and then helped her sit in the end chair.

"Mama," was all Maddie could manage. She began to cry.

"What's happened, are you all right? Beau, the children?" Annie held Maddie's face in her hands.

"Mama," Maddie gasped. "Beau shot Barney. It's…it's bad."

A black flash rolled across Annie's brain. She lost her balance and sank to her knees in front of her daughter. Her head dropped into Maddie's lap.

"Mama, are you all right? Mama!" Maddie shook Annie's shoulders.

"Is he?" Annie managed to whisper.

"No, but he took five in the chest. It's bad, Mama."

Boots stepped across the floor, but Annie couldn't raise her head. Large hands cupped her elbows and helped her to her feet. She looked into Beau's face. His mouth moved, but she couldn't hear anything. "What, what did you say?"

"Mother, he reached for his gun, well, I thought it

was his gun. I had to shoot him. I'm sorry, but it couldn't be helped. You know he draws at anyone and anything. I really thought he'd shoot me." Beau hung his head.

Her knees buckled, but Beau kept her from falling. The sound of the bell, boots, and voices began to fill the hotel. Annie found her legs, and her voice. "Bring him here."

The next half hour blurred into a tunnel of activity. Annie fought dizzy blackness to give directions. "Maddie, boil water. Beau, you better get the sheriff, somebody pull the covers off the bed in the north corner room." No use calling for a doctor. There hadn't been a regular medical man since the Ninth and Tenth Cavalry left Fort Stockton in eighty-seven.

Her son, Thad, and Barney's friend, Charlie Simmons, carried him in. She pushed down a scream, and with her hand over her mouth, she led them to the room. Barney was covered in blood and gasped for breath.

They laid him on the bed. Barney writhed in pain. He opened his eyes and looked at Annie. For the first time since she'd known him, she saw fear in his eyes. She stood frozen in the doorway.

"I'll undress him, Mama." Thad stepped toward his step-father on the bed.

"No, you go with Beau to the sheriff. I take it you saw it happen?" She steadied herself with one hand on the door frame.

"Yes, ma'am, a lot of people did," Thad said, stepping aside. "Barney did reach, but he had no gun.

It was his cane."

"I'll go too, and tell what really happened," Charlie seethed. He rushed out of the room, his boots stomped through the hotel, the bell dinged, and then the door slammed. It seemed to play out in slow motion. She couldn't focus.

"It was Barney reached first, Mama. Beau didn't have a choice, especially after the way Barney's been threatening to shoot him," Thad said.

Annie nodded. "Get on with you, now."

Thad turned back toward his stepfather and knelt beside him. He took Barney's hand.

"Good man," Barney whispered and then groaned.

Thad cleared his throat, squeezed Barney's hand, and then turned to Annie. "I'll send my Sarah to come and help."

Annie braced herself with both arms in the door frame. She swallowed a sob and took a deep breath. She felt hands on her shoulders.

"I'm so sorry, Mama." Maddie turned Annie around and embraced her.

Annie leaned into her daughter's embrace, and then pushed away. *No. I can't let go. Not yet.* "Please take those biscuits out of the oven, and when Sarah gets here tell her to take them and that ham I was slicing over to the school. I can't have those children in here today. Bring me a pan of hot water, and some rags."

Maddie nodded, and left Annie alone.

Annie pressed her lips together and willed steel into her mind, then walked into the room. "Well, you really did it this time." She knelt and began tearing at his shirt.

"I," he began, but fell into a fit of coughing, blood spattering his mouth. He finally nodded.

It took some doing, and he hollered the whole time, but she got his shirt and his belt off.

Maddie brought in the water and rags but left.

Barney quieted a little as she dabbed at his wounds with the warm cloths. Had Beau missed his heart? Still, he looked to be bleeding out. She cleaned him up as best she could, tried to apply pressure, and wrapped his chest good and tight.

"Send for the priest, Annie," Barney whispered.

"There's not a priest in town now, Barney."

She'd been secretly glad there'd not been a regular priest available to pass judgment on two divorces, but now she'd give anything for a Father to say Last Rites. Barney had never done anything but laugh at her for praying the Rosary. Then again, she'd never known him to be afraid before. Could the weight of killing seven men finally be bothering him?

"He never kilt nobody but that didn't need killin'," Charlie was fond of saying. Barney could do no wrong in his eyes since he'd saved Charlie's life.

"Annie, take it down." Barney labored over every word.

Annie knew what he meant. She reached up, pulled the pins from her hair, and let it fall across her shoulders. She held his hand and leaned close to him.

"Molasses," he said, and tried to stroke her hair, wincing with every motion.

"Barney," she said, and let the tears come.

He took a deep breath, well, as deep as he could, and tried to sit up.

"No. Lie still. It'll be better that way. Please, Barney," she said.

"Annie, I don't want to die like this. It's about to overtake me. The pain."

She pulled his hand to her cheek, bathing it in her tears. The one thing that caused Barney the most trouble was the only thing that could help him physically now. Would he call on the only thing that could help his death?

"Maddie," she called.

She must have been hovering near for she answered almost immediately, "Yes, ma'am?"

"See if there's a bottle of whiskey in the room where that cowboy is staying. They know they're not supposed to bring it in the hotel, but they do it anyway."

"All right." A few minutes later she returned with a half-full bottle of whiskey.

Annie held his head up a bit and tried to give him a drink.

He could only sip a bit at a time, not nearly enough to help with the pain. It only caused a fit of coughing and his breathing became more labored. "I just want peace, Annie, do you still have it?"

She reached into her pocket and felt the cold steel.

CHAPTER 2

Annie walked toward the kitchen the next morning, bent on starting breakfast. Horses stampeded in her head, and her heart felt squeezed like a dirty dish rag. Her family filled the dining room. Baby Gene toddled out of Maddie's arms and wrapped his arms around her knees. She picked him up and he nuzzled his face into her neck. *Poor thing, he doesn't understand what's happened.* Mavis clung to her Uncle Thad, crying with little gasps of breath that broke Annie's heart anew. Mavis loved her father, but often said in her five-year-old lisp, "He scare me, Mama." Junior stood next to Thad with his lips in a grim line. Her son could not fool anyone, for his red eyes told the story.

"Mother, I sent a telegram to Liza Mae," Thad said. Her third child, Liza Mae in San Angelo was not well, and Annie hurt worse knowing her daughter would likely not be able to come. "I'll drive out to the ranch and bring Jack and the girls home."

Jack, born after Liza Mae and only twenty, did not like Barney much. They'd argued many times over Barney's treatment of Annie. He spent as much time away from Fort Stockton as he could, helping the judge on the ranch. He'd taken his teen sisters, Evelyn and Myra with him. Her children from her first marriage, even though they sometimes didn't care for their stepfather, would rally around her. Thad, her oldest son, was the exception. He seemed to get along with Barney quite well.

"Mother, you do not have to make biscuits today. Aunt Mary and I can handle this. They won't be as good as yours, of course, but please, you need your rest." Maddie took off her crocheted shawl and wrapped it around Annie's shoulders.

Gratitude filled her heart to see that Maddie, and Annie's younger sister Mary, had breakfast well underway. A shooting would not stop the daily operations of any business, They were common occurrences in Fort Stockton. This event did cause a sensation because it was the famous, or rather infamous, Barney Riggs. Still, hotel guests would be wanting their breakfast. Things galloped on as usual, while her heart nearly burst with pain. If she didn't find some work to do, she'd go crazy. She looked around the room at her loving family so willing to be there for her, but suddenly felt very alone. The future of this family was now on her shoulders, hers alone. The weight of it made her arms and legs feel very weak, and too heavy to bear. She put Gene down on the floor.

"Come on fella," Thad said, picking Gene up. "Let's go feed the horses." He took Mavis by the hand, and nodded toward Junior to come along.

They went to the front door in the foyer. Junior stood facing her, his features contorted. Tears sprang from his eyes.

Annie dropped to her knees and held out her arms. He ran to her and sobbed. She wanted to let go, to cry with him, but if she did she would lose her mind. She just held him tight for a long moment. "Go on now, go with Uncle Thad." Junior took a deep breath and then ran out the front door. Annie felt faint.

"Can I fix you a cup of coffee, Annie?" Mary put her arm around her, pulled her to a stand, and then kissed her cheek.

"Yes, that's a good idea," Maddie said. "Aunt Mary, why don't you take Mother to her room, and I'll bring a little coffee and toast."

The room where Barney died, and where Annie had been allowed a personal space as manager of the hotel, was her only link to him now. Just hours before he'd been alive. She hadn't let anyone help her clean the aftermath of his injuries. It was Barney's blood, her Barney. He'd spent many a night there with her when she'd stayed over night for work.

Annie let herself be guided back to the room. Mary settled her in her rocking chair, the one Barney had sent from Sears and Roebuck. She let Mary wrap the shawl more tightly around her. It felt a little like Barney's arms. Mary put a spare blanket on her lap and tucked it around her legs.

Maddie brought in a tray of coffee and toast. She set it next to Annie on an ornate lamp table, another gift from Barney.

"Thank you," Annie whispered, as the girls tiptoed out of the room, but she was already somewhere else in her mind.

Why did it always end in destruction? The violent lifestyle of Pecos County crowded into her happiness once again, as it had her entire life before Barney and during their marriage. What did the future hold? Why keep trying?

Her Heavenly Father seemed so far away. She remembered the violent shooting of two Mexican men she'd witnessed when only a child. She had no idea of the reason, but she'd never forget them being buried with no marker. Did anyone but her remember them when the town started building up over the unmarked graves?

She dozed fitfully as memories washed over her. Perhaps her faith had run out, used up over so many heartaches, because she couldn't feel God.

Somehow, she'd managed to believe and go on when her brother John was killed in a useless brawl at a dance. His youthful face morphed into a corpse and jolted her awake. Would it never end?

She'd married James Johnson way too young. She'd borne him six children in succession while dealing with his drunken behavior. All her trying only resulted in his simply disappearing one day. Gone, just gone.

Tears came and she couldn't stop them. She didn't want to worry the family, but she didn't feel she could go on. She stood and stumbled into bed, nearly tripping over the blanket as it fell from her lap. She wrapped herself around Barney's pillow and wept.

Maddie tiptoed in to check on her. "Mother, please, let me cover you up." Maddie removed Annie's slippers, covered her with the bedclothes and then wiped her brow with a cool cloth. "Here, here's some water, please, Mother, take a drink."

"The little ones?" Annie whispered, her throat dry and raspy.

"Doña Piña and the Hijas of Mary are taking care of them, so that Thad and Sarah can take care of the arrangements. They are well in hand, don't worry."

Annie raised her head long enough to take a few sips of water. She tasted liquid laced with Mrs. Winslow's Soothing Syrup. Perhaps it would help her sleep deeply enough that the memories would stop.

After setting the water glass on the nightstand, Maddie lay down next to Annie and put her arm over her mother's shoulders. Her sister appeared in the doorway just as Annie felt the sleep begin to overtake her. Maddie whispered something, and then darkness.

This pattern continued for two days as Annie vacillated between grief and sleep. Several times she awoke to find her youngest children, Junior, Errol, Mavis, and Gene kneeling beside her bed. She'd caress their little faces and try to smile, but sleep would overtake her again.

Annie awoke the third morning with the dread that she would lose her job. Maddie had assured her that Mr. Kettler insisted Annie take all the time she needed. Maddie and Mary could handle the hotel. How long had she been languishing there? She shook the groggy sleep from her eyes.

Her friend, Doña Matilde, was on her knees beside her bed. She prayed the Rosary aloud, one hand on the beads, and the other rested on Annie's leg.

Annie forced herself to sit up and bowed her head. The soothing sound of her friend's voice calmed Annie, but her head ached with the gallop of a herd of horses.

When the Rosary was complete, Doña Matilde looked up at her and offered a sympathetic, toothless smile, her white-gray hair pulled back into her usual tight, severe bun. Her thin, wrinkled arms reached for Annie. Always so plain and wearing a nun's garb, but her eyes shone with the light of the Gospel. "Mija, you will be all right."

Doubtful, but Annie returned the loving smile as best she could. "How long have I been here?'

"A couple of days, my child. You've been reliving your entire life out loud."

Yes. That much she could remember but didn't realize it could be heard. "The children?"

"Your lawyer friend, Mr. Jamison, has taken them out to his ranch to play with his children for the weekend. He and Mrs. Jamison will take good care of them. They will return when he comes back to town on Monday."

"What day is it?"

"Sunday morning, mija. Shall we get a bath and get dressed?"

Annie didn't want to do either. She didn't answer.

After a few minutes of silence, Doña Matilde said, "I've learned things about the Miller Feud I didn't know, that you had to wear an iron vest if you went out after Barney killed a few of them in Pecos. How uncomfortable."

"Yes, that was another time that Henson Jamison took the children out to his ranch. There was fear of retaliation."

"Yes, and that was the time the tide began to turn for Barney's reputation. Remember he changed from outlaw to lawman after that."

Doña Matilde always made Annie want to say, "The sky is blue," to see how she would counter, because Doña tried to put a positive spin on things. She always pointed Annie to Christ. No matter what Annie said in complaint, Doña Matilde found a way to turn it around. Her friend's influence had changed her over the years, but now there was no point in trying to help. As usual, everything ended in death and destruction.

"Do you think you survived so many things for naught?"

Could the dear old woman read her mind?

"To what end, my friend? I've watched this town grow from nothing to a thriving community that still relies on the gun to settle its differences. My children will grow up in the shadow of murder and revenge.

"It's still hard to teach the practices of the church. If it were not for you, I'd never have found my faith. We have no priest to serve at St. Joseph's and only a small school whose teacher is only here looking for a husband. History repeats itself, and all my prayers have come to nothing."

Doña Matilde's eyes shone with tears. She cast her glance at Annie for a moment and then whispered, "And?"

Annie closed her eyes and tried to enter the realm

of blessings. Doña Matilde had played this game with her from the time she was a child. "And we walk more safely on the streets since Barney put down the Miller Gang."

Doña Matilde nodded.

"And I have eleven wonderful children."

Doña Matilde smiled and nodded. "And," she continued, waiting for more.

"And we have taught the young women of Fort Stockton about Christ and formed the service group, The Hijas de Maria."

Her toothless smiled widened, and Doña Matilde clasped her hands under her chin.

Annie continued, "And we all work, go to school, worship, and celebrate together." Small consolation, but her heart felt a tiny bit lighter. Even if she could put it all behind her, her whole being ached for Barney. *Could anyone understand? She loved him so much, but their marriage was impossible.*

"Come, my child." Doña Matilde motioned Annie to get on her knees beside her.

Annie obeyed.

Doña Matilde made an imaginary square in the air. "Here is a box. It is the box of your past. We will put everything in it, no?"

Annie stared at the imaginary box. Where to begin?

"I'll start," Doña Matilde said. She fisted one hand as if she held something. "The unkind and tragic things you saw as a child." She pretended to put them in the box.

Annie pretended to hold something in her hand. "The night that John was killed." She put it in the box. Tears streamed down her face. "When James left me with six children to raise on my own." She dropped that in the box.

"When Sheriff Royal was killed and Barney was accused of pulling the trigger," Annie said. *One man Barney actually didn't kill.*

Doña Matilde put her arm around Annie as she dredged up every heartache she could think of and put them in the imaginary box.

"I think you've filled it, mija. We will close it and tie up with a ribbon." Doña Matilde feigned closing the box and mimicked tying it up and finished with a bow.

"Now, we will give it to the Father. It will be in His safe keeping. You can trust that He will handle your heartache in the best way possible and you don't need it anymore. Trust Him, my Annie. Take hold of it."

Annie took hold of the box, which she could almost truly see now.

"Lift it up, and He will take it."

Annie lifted the box, and with a slight shove, tossed it into the air and imagined it floating like a soft chicken feather. In her mind's eye it disappeared.

Exhaustion and a measure of peace settled on Annie's spirit.

"You must sleep now, mija. I will pray it will be a dreamless sleep. When you awaken, we will start filling a Blessing Box, which will keep your heart in the right place as you pursue your dreams." She tucked

Annie into bed, settled her hand on Annie's forehead and prayed in Spanish.

Annie fell into a soft darkness.

CHAPTER 3

It took a year, but Annie received Barney's estate. She counted out the cash in her hand, $4,876.00. She'd never held that much money before, but she knew exactly what to do with it. She wanted to hang on to it and feel rich for a day or two but she needed to move fast. Mr. Herman Kettler wanted to relocate and was keen to sell the hotel. He'd left Fort Stockton to scout a new location for another hotel. He'd left his younger brother, Percival Kettler, in charge of the sale. If she could get her hands on it, her dream would come true. She put the money in her apron pocket and walked down the hill and over the bridge to the Kettler Store.

"Is Mr. Kettler in?" she asked as she pushed open the heavy wooden door.

"He is supposed to come and relieve me in a few minutes, if you'd like to wait." Abel continued to stock the shelves with supplies procured from the supply wagons that had just come and gone. Boxes and muslin bags tumbled all over the floor. Susanna Martin had still not cut off those long blond curls of his.

"Here, let me help you," she said.

"Aw, Mrs. Annie, you don't have to do that," Abel said, but he didn't stop her when she picked up fifty-pound bags of flour and stacked them in their usual place against the wall in the back.

"How's your mother, Abel?" she asked.

Abel let a sigh escape his lips. "She's getting awfully tired. She says it's nearly time." The boy looked positively exhausted.

Mr. Kettler tromped in, his boots assaulting the wooden floor. He scrunched his beady brown eyes into a scowl at the sight before him.

"I pay you a fair wage for managing the hotel but stacking heavy packages in my store is another thing altogether. Abel, how can you let Mrs. Riggs handle these heavy bags?"

Your brother's store, mind you. As if I don't do it all day at the hotel. "Oh, don't jaw at him. I wanted to do it. Just killing the time until you got here. May I have a moment?" Annie asked, brushing the flour from her hands and skirt.

"Yes, of course," he said.

Annie followed him into the office in the back of the store. She waited for him to maneuver his considerable middle around his desk and settle into his large black leather chair. He took off his black bowler and tossed it to the coat rack by the door. She found it hard to repress a giggle because the small line of hair he had from ear to ear, none on top, stuck out on all sides.

"Please, sit down Annie," he said, pointing her to a nearby straight-back chair.

She took a deep breath to steady herself, but the smell of cigar and whiskey stung her throat and nose. "I want," she began but coughed instead. She reached into her apron pocket for her handkerchief and pressed it to her mouth until the cough subsided. "I want to buy the hotel, Sir. I understand the price is $4000 dollars, and I have the money in hand. We could make the deal today." Her attempt at a business-like demeanor turned into a giddy smile. She couldn't help it.

"Ah, so you did receive Mr. Riggs's assets. Well, good for you. I'd be happy to sell you the hotel, Annie, if," he said, and leaned back in his chair. "Well, if you had a husband. There's no one who can run it better than you, of course, but by law you'd have to have a man sign the deed. Without a husband, I don't know how you could handle that." He slung both legs on top of his desk and crossed his feet at the ankles, dirt from the road falling from his boots. He twisted his arms across his chest in a firm dismissal of her request.

"But why? I have the cash right here in my pocket, and," she began.

A tall man she didn't recognize walked into the office without knocking, and Annie clamped her mouth shut. Last thing she needed was to have a stranger know she had $4,000 dollars on her person.

The stranger completely ignored Annie but tipped his Stetson at Mr. Kettler. "I've come to see if you've considered my offer to buy the hotel."

Mr. Kettler stood and wiggled around his desk and shook the man's hand. "Mr. Freeman. Ah, you've made the trip from Pecos, and I'm not ready to make a decision. Would you wait outside for me a moment?"

The man straightened his small bow tie, sniffed a

slight disdain at Annie, but then nodded. Mr. Kettler closed the door behind him.

Annie squirmed in her seat.

He stepped even closer to Annie. He stood right over her, his acrid cigar breath turning her stomach. "You know, if we were married, the hotel would be yours, ours, and you could keep your money," he said.

Annie stood, stepped back, and fisted her hips. "Mr. Kettler, a husband is the last thing I will ever need again. Now I came here to negotiate a legitimate business deal with you, and you want to be silly. You're no more interested in me than I am in you." Free labor, likely? He'd never shown any interest before. His brother had been fair in his dealings with her and had shown sincere appreciation for the way she ran the hotel. But this man? She was certain he'd only just thought of it.

Her throat constricted. The man in the Stetson could probably give him more than $4000. She shouldn't have been so harsh.

She softened her voice and clasped her hands together. "Mr. Kettler. I have eleven children. Some of them married, with children who also depend on me. I intend to help them all get a good start in life. I don't know if your personal offer includes the package deal that is An-, *Mrs.* Annie Riggs."

Percival Kettler tossed his head back with a wide-eyed expression. His cheeks flushed crimson.

No, she could see he hadn't thought of that.

He reached for his hat from the rack, put it on, and stepped around her. "If you can find a man to do your business for you, then it's a deal, but no woman will sign a deed of sale. I'll give you two days, because my brother thinks very highly of you, and then if you can't come up with a male partner, I'm selling to the man from Pecos." He left the room.

Annie sat in his office a few moments collecting herself. Why couldn't she just buy the hotel if she had the money? Bessie at the Comfort Arms down Main Street didn't have to have a man sign for her, although she had to have multiple men, and painted girls, in order to do her business. The Riggs Hotel would be respectable. Nobody minded if she worked her fingers to the bone, but to succeed, get ahead; nobody wanted that for her.

She would just go back to the hotel and think about it. If she appealed to him once more then perhaps he might break down and waive the stupid rule. But, more likely, if she didn't comply with his wishes, she'd lose her chance. Annie walked back down the hill to the hotel, letting the soft Spring breeze calm her.

She ruminated over it as she prepared dinner for the guests. She wanted to make a specially seasoned roast for Henson Jamison. Maybe her friend would have an idea.

When Henson came in, she took his Stetson hat and walked into the dining room with him. He sat down and she began to serve him. Most patrons fixed their own plate at the buffet, but Henson was her friend, and she often took her meals with him. He rented a room at the hotel with an outside entrance for his law office. After he ate, she sat down and served coffee.

The other guests retired to their rooms.

Some of the men headed over to the Grey Mule Saloon.

"Now Mrs. Annie girl, you're awfully quiet. Something on your mind? What's troubling you, my friend?"

She pulled the money out of her pocket and laid it on the table. "I want to buy the hotel, and that money right there is enough."

"Well, I'll be. I can't think of a better idea. First," he said, looking from side to side, "put that money back in your pocket. Second, why don't you just do it?"

"Because Mr. Kettler, the younger, won't let me sign the bill of sale. He says I have to have a man to do it."

"Tarnation! Well, it's still illegal in some states, but you can do it in Texas. I guess Kettler is set in his ways."

"He even offered to marry me; can you believe that? He changed his mind pretty quick when I mentioned my children."

Henson threw his head back and laughed. "That old coot. How humiliating."

She loved how Henson seemed to understand her. She'd often wished that he'd move Hepatica and their children into town. But their stake wouldn't be his for another year.

"I can't believe it. Say, why don't I sign it, then I'll deed it over to you. That will be legally binding, and you can get around Kettler's old stodgy ideas."

"Henson Jamison, you'd do that for me? You'd be the only one I'd trust with this." How providential to have a friend who was also a lawyer.

"It's the least I can do. You have weathered more heartache and trouble than many a woman combined. You've done a good job with this hotel and been a good friend to Heppie and me. I think it would be an excellent investment for your family. You'd have to work hard. But then you always have." He wiped his mouth with his napkin and stood. "I'll speak to him right away."

Annie smiled from ear to ear. She took the money out of her pocket and placed it in his hands, "Thanks, Henson."

"It'll take a day or two, but I'll let you know when it's done; then I'll draw up an official Transfer of Ownership via Gift. You'll be a hotel owner, Mrs. Annie Stella Frazer Johnson Riggs." He bowed low.

Annie felt overwhelmed. She jumped up and kissed him on the cheek. She hoped Hepatica wouldn't mind. After this, they'd have nothing but the best any time they ever came into the hotel.

Excitement carried her through the next two days. On the third day, Annie received a message delivered by Abel Marten that Henson had secured the property and that he'd be coming by to see her that evening when he returned from the ranch.

She gathered her children and friends and threw a celebration party. Henson came in and showed her the bill of sale, and then the paper that signed it over to her. She signed the document, and nearly ruined the ink when a tear plopped down on the paper as she wrote her name.

Suddenly the sound of cheering went up in the room "Hip, hip, hooray! For she's a jolly good fellow!" They celebrated into the night and included any hotel guest who heard the commotion and came in to see what was going on. Beau and Maddie presided over everything, serving and keeping glasses full of lemonade.

The sound of stomping boots brought the reveling to a stop. "What's this?" Charlie Simmons spat out as he entered the dining room.

"Mrs. Riggs has bought the hotel, we are celebrating!" Henson said, offering him a glass of lemonade.

Charlie knocked the glass from Henson's hand, lemonade splashing everywhere. He put his hand on his gun. and his face turned red as he turned toward Annie. "And I guess you bought it with your blood money. Poor Barney, he'd be alive today if you didn't have this scheme."

Beau Chadwick stepped toward him.

"Go ahead, why not shoot me too? She may pay you to do it like she did my best friend, but you'll not get anything from me." Charlie turned suddenly and rushed out of the room.

"What's that all about?" one of the new hotel guests asked.

"Oh, old Charlie is just drunk, and he thinks Mrs. Riggs deliberately had her husband shot," Henson said. "Barney Riggs saved his life in that Yuma prison riot, and Charlie cared for him quite a lot. He seems to turn his eyes and ears from the truth about Barney's drinking and the way he treated Mrs. Riggs."

Maddie brought cloths from the kitchen and then knelt and wiped the lemonade from the floor.

The room fell awkwardly silent for a half a minute.

"Mama, we're so proud of you. And we'll all help you as much as we can," Maddie said to the applause of all present.

"I'll need all the help I can get. The hotel is mine, free and clear, but it will take a great deal of hard work. Thank you, my family. I'm truly grateful."

As everyone dispersed and walked around her newly acquired property, Annie helped Beau and Maddie clean up the remains of the party, and then went to the parlor. She began to play a soft melody on the piano that Barney bought for her and had sent all the way from San Angelo. She closed her eyes and prayed her thanks to heaven. Tears poured down her cheeks as she confessed to herself that she'd rather have Barney than his money, but as cantankerous as he was in the settlement dispute, which was just his way of trying to get her back, he'd want her to find a way to take care of their children and grandchildren.

That would be the focus of her life. She would create a new life for herself and find a way to make sure that Barney's legacy was not only remembered as one of violence, but also one of generosity, and through his children, one of integrity, faith, strength, purpose, and success.

Her family slipped back into the parlor and were quietly listening to the music.

Annie stopped playing.

Maddie put her arms around Annie. "Please don't stop. It's beautiful. Something feels better after all these months of hardship and heartache."

Annie looked around the room at her blended family. Mary rocked baby Gene, who was snoozing in spite of the noisy party. Errol, Mavis and Junior sat cross legged on the floor. Maddie and Beau sat down on the settee. Thad and Sarah stood by the door. The few hotel guests who'd joined in bid them all goodnight.

Annie couldn't play now, her hands shook as gratitude washed over her.

"You know," Thad said, "Barney could tell a joke. It was so funny the way he tried to leave out the cuss words. It would totally take out the meaning, but he would laugh and laugh."

They all nodded and laughed.

Annie just shook her head thinking about Barney's efforts to interact with his children.

Mavis still cried over her father's death. "I loved it when he rode me on his back, acting like he was my horse. The men at the saloon laughed at him as we went by, but he didn't care."

"He always gave us money for new dresses," Evelyn said.

"Yes," Myra laughed. "Even when Mama said 'No.'"

Thad talked of how Barney had taken him and

Jack hunting, taught them how to take care of their horses, and helped him out when he wanted to get married. Jack, despite his differences with Barney, nodded in agreement. The Johnson part of the family reminiscened fondly with the Riggs. Her heart swelled with pride. Maybe she'd had an influence on her children. What a blessing to hear them focus on their father's strengths, and not on what had no doubt frustrated and frightened them. She turned back to the piano.

She began to sing, and they all joined in the chorus of that old civil war song, "The Vacant Chair."

"We shall meet, but we shall miss him..."

CHAPTER 4

Charlie Simmons stood in the doorway of the Grey Mule Saloon seething and spitting tobacco.

Across the street a crew of men lowered the Kettler Hotel sign from the high dormer with rope. The newly painted Riggs Hotel sign rested against the building, ready to replace it. The horses tied to the rail in front of the saloon whickered. Their owners stood about and watched.

"Blood money," he mumbled under his breath. "She took Barney's money and bought that hotel. Money she got from having him killed." He kicked the dust.

"You better get that bald head of yorn back in here. Beau Chadwick is over there, and he might just as well shoot you as anybody," Cal Gibbs said.

Chadwick, having been accepted into the Texas Rangers in New Mexico, would be leaving soon.

Charlie was secretly relieved about that. He turned and jabbed his finger at Cal. "Yeah, shoot a man in cold blood and they promote you to Texas Ranger. I ain't afraid of him. Nobody asked no sheepherder for no opinion. You wanna keep drinkin' in here, keep your maw shut."

Cal laughed.

Charlie came inside and shut the door.

The sheriff stood over there too, and he'd already warned Charlie about spoutin' his mouth off at Annie Riggs.

It was a cryin' shame, that's what it was. No better man than Barney Riggs had ever walked the dirt roads of Fort Stockton. That wicked woman had him killed, he was sure of it.

"What's it to you after all this time? What's it been, two years? Who else was the judge gonna award his assets to? He didn't leave no will, I heard."

"Shut it!" Charlie yelled and put his hand on his gun.

"Come off it. What's the matter, Charlie? I know you two were pretty thick. I once overheard Barney in here, drunk on his face, promise you some of his property. You thought he really meant it, didn't you? He died before you could get your hands on it." Cal snickered, downed his shot, and stood to leave.

"Good riddance," Charlie said, and let the door slam behind him.

Truth was, Barney had promised him a piece of land. Charlie had no proof. He thought about talking to Annie about it but couldn't get past his hatred of her. He'd find a way to get his due, even if he had to take it by force.

A young stranger came into the saloon, looked around, and then choose a seat by the front window. "What's going on over there?" He took off his hat, balanced it on his knee, and then ran a hand through short-cropped brown hair.

"Highway robbery, or rather murder," Charlie said. He watched from the window on the other side of the door. It's not right." And that Beau Chadwick got to go free. No justice in this world.

Annie came out on the veranda. She walked down the stairs to the street and looked up to watch the work. Beau and Maddie joined her.

"Look at that. New duds and hat for the occasion. She don't mind spendin' his money," Charlie said. "She must think she's royalty with that purple dress, and those feathers in her hat."

"That's Barney Riggs's wife?" the stranger said, gawking.

"Yep, standing with Beau Chadwick, the man she paid to kill him. What's your interest?" Charlie asked and walked over to the whiskey barrel that served as a table for the newcomer.

"Just curious. Is she packin' in that apron pocket?"

"I wouldn't speculate what's in that pocket, but if you ever see her put her hand in, you better run or draw. You gonna order a drink, or did you just come in here to watch the treachery?"

Charlie looked hard at the tall, youthful man. Something familiar registered in his brain. "What's your name, mister?"

"Frank Jennings," he said, never taking his gaze off the doings across the street.

Realization energized Charlie as he leaned down for a better look. "Yeah, you look just like your daddy. You're John Jennings' boy."

Frank started and shoved his chair back a few

inches. "How do you know my pa?"

"From Yuma prison. I knew him, and I know Barney Riggs shot him dead. I was there."

"Riggs was a friend of yours?" Frank Jennings stood and put his hand on his gun.

"Best friend, but don't worry, I ain't got no quarrel with you, and if I guess right about why you're here, you ain't got one with me." Charlie said and pulled a chair up to the barrel. He stared at Frank, and Frank stared back. Charlie looked out the window, then caught Frank's gaze again. He felt as if he eavesdropped on the stranger's thoughts.

"He killed my pa, and made life miserable for my mother."

"He did kill your pa. Shame you can't get your revenge on him. He got hisself shot dead, and it was at Annie Riggs's bidding. She wanted a divorce, and he wouldn't give it to her without a fight."

Frank stood, pulled his gun from the holster, and started for the door.

"You ain't too smart, are you. You kill her now with all those people looking on and you'll be slapped in jail and then prison, if you ain't shot first. That won't help your ma," Charlie said. *And I won't get my land.* "I got a better idea, but it'll take some time."

Frank returned his gun to his holster, and sat down.

"I wouldn't use your real name around these parts. Barney Riggs is a hero here, and folks know every detail of the Yuma incident," Charlie said.

Frank nodded. "Gotta cousin name of Hankins."

"Frank Hankins it is, then."

"She's the widow of your best friend," Frank said. He stood and placed his hat on his head.

Charlie raised to his full five-feet four-inch height. "She killed him. Don't leave me out of it. Oh, and you better leave that gun here with me. She hates guns."

"But she's packing in that apron," Frank said, peering out the window again.

"I wouldn't risk it if I was you," Charlie replied.

The two men talked long into the night.

CHAPTER 5

Annie carefully lettered a poster for the entrance of the hotel. She'd learned a great deal from working for Mr. Kettler and knew exactly what kind of hotel she wanted to run. As an employee she'd had to clean up nasty spittle, break up fights, and try to rouse drunken cowboys from her beds.

Riggs Hotel Rules

Guests without baggage must pay in advance.

No account carried longer than one week.

All boisterous and profane language strictly forbidden.

All drinking or gambling in rooms strictly forbidden.

Please do not spit or throw ashes or matches on the floor.

Guests wishing early calls must notify clerk before retiring.

Damage to furniture, other than ordinary wear, will be charged to occupants of rooms.

Guests must refrain from all singing or loud talking after reasonable hours for retiring.

Persons engaging rooms will be charged from time rooms are placed at their disposal to departure whether occupied or not.

Please extinguish lights on leaving rooms or retiring. Extra charge for burning lights unnecessarily.

It is expected that parents will exercise proper care over children and not allow them to make a playground of halls and parlors.

Money, jewels, and valuables must be left with clerk in the office, otherwise proprietor will not be responsible for any loss.

Meals a la carte from 6:00 AM to 10:30 PM

She tacked the poster to the wall, just inside the entrance, then stepped back to take a good look. Nice and straight. She allowed a smile as she looked around the hotel foyer. The early morning light cast a shine on the gleaming wood of the check-in counter. Beautiful. Sometimes she couldn't contain her gratitude. She whispered a prayer of thanks, and then took a deep breath against the day to come.

There'd be wide-eyed surprise at the way she'd outfitted her blouse. The first few weeks as owner and proprietor of the Riggs Hotel, she'd worn her best dresses and hats. But even with Maddie's help, cooking and cleaning had wreaked havoc on her clothes. She'd shortened the sleeves on her green checked blouse, repositioning the ruffle at the elbow. Annie's brushed twill skirt in black was protected by her white cotton apron. Might as well be comfortable.

The ladies that thought themselves fashionable and pious had whispered when she didn't wear widow's weeds after Barney died. Why should she? And how was she to move forward if she commemorated his death every day in a constricting, hot black dress?

Oh, they'd talked enough when she'd decided to

marry him in the first place. Already divorced from James Johnson and raising six of his children alone, she'd been the subject of their gossip for some time.

She buttoned the top button of her blouse. She'd likely unbutton it again during the heat of the afternoon, but for now she would start the day as smart as a working woman could. Her reflection in the front door glass revealed a stray strand of hair which she tucked behind her ear. Her hand rested on the smooth wood surface of the counter. How proud Barney would have been back in the day, before he turned mean. He'd put his hat on her head, and tweak her nose, his gray eyes shining with a twinkle. He'd have broken his back to help her get ready.

Her eyes stung with tears that she could not allow to fall. Her efforts to remember the good times could not be separated from the bad, try as she might. With a click of her tongue she tried to squash the thought that yes, in the morning he'd be proud and sweet and hardworking, but in the evening he'd have tried to ruin it all with the bottle.

Time to start a batch of biscuits. Those cowboys surely loved them, and she didn't mind obliging. Townsfolk came to the hotel just for meals, which really added to her income. She kept beans, biscuits, and ham for the cowboys and sheep men.

Thank heaven for Maddie's help. She checked in the guests and organized the cleaning of the rooms. What would she do when Maddie left to join Beau in New Mexico? Her daughters, Evelyn and Myra, had offered help, but Annie hated to curtail their school activities. Callie did the laundry now for all the guests as well as for the family. Perhaps she could teach Callie to cook for guests. Thad and Sarah had moved to San Angelo to help Liza Mae. Liza's health had improved, but her husband had left her. Why couldn't they all just move home?

Maddie walked into the kitchen, a young man following. "Mama, this is Frank Hankins. He's booked a bed and board for the week. He also asked if we needed any help."

Annie dried her hands on the rag tucked into her apron waist and offered this tall young man a hand. What was he, early twenties?

He shook it, but never made eye contact. *What's the boy up to, or is he just shy?* She quelled the thought. "What brings you to Fort Stockton?"

"Just passin' through to visit family in San Angelo. Thought I'd stop for a while, let my horse rest, and maybe take in a job and earn a little more money. Don't want to show up empty handed at my Aunt Phoebe's. She's been real sick." He held his hat in his hand and looked at the floor.

"What kind of job are you looking for?" Annie stepped back around the table and continued rolling biscuits. Barney's voice chided in her thoughts, *Stop takin' in strays.*

"Just about anything. I'm good with my hands, can build things, and can fix just about anything havin' to do with wood." He ventured a quick look into her eyes and pulled his lips in. His blue eyes squinted, as though he were about to dodge a bullet.

"I see. Well, I got an old cabin out back where my laundress Callie stays. It's falling apart. Go on out there and see if you can fix it. If you're a mind to, I'll pay you to get it in shape for Callie."

Ah, the help she'd prayed for. If this worked out, it would help. Her son, Jack, could usually be counted on for carpentry, but he'd joined a cattle drive. His wanderlust got the better of him.

"Yes, ma'am," he said.

Annie showed him to the back door, and then she returned to her biscuits.

The way the boy looked down to the floor seemed more like sadness than shyness. He'd slumped his shoulders over, and it seemed to Annie that it indicated fear. What was that boy's story? She cut the dough and slid the biscuits in the oven.

Frank came back in the kitchen. "I can patch that roof for sure. The door is coming off its hinges, and I can fix that. There are some loose boards all the way around. I'm your man, Mrs. Riggs." He looked directly at her with a desperate expression.

Desperation fueled by some kind of hurt. She'd seen it before. Barney never got over his hurt, and he was just about this boy's age when it happened. Barney was the love of her life, but he never got over his first wife cheating on him. He'd murdered her lover because of it and landed in Yuma Prison.

"You can board your horse at the stables on the other side of the saloon," she said. "Let me show you to your room." She put down the rolling pin and wiped her hands as she walked out of the kitchen. She looked back to see Frank Hankins standing right where she left him. He glanced around the kitchen as if he might be trying to find a place to escape.

"You want a room or don't you?" She nodded toward the courtyard.

He followed. His boots thumped across the floor with a long, slow gait. Annie unlocked the door to the first room past the kitchen. "It's yours alone for now. All the other rooms are rented. No tellin' who you'll have to share the bed with by day's end."

"I don't mind. When would you like me to start on the work?" He pushed on the mattress and bounced it a bit.

She couldn't discern what he thought about it. His eyes drooped. He must be tired.

"Let's wait until after breakfast tomorrow. Callie does the laundry then, so she'll be out of the cabin."

"Yes, ma'am."

"Food's on the sideboard in the dining room. It's simple, but plenty of it."

"Yes, ma'am."

Polite, almost too polite.

"Well, I'll leave you to get settled."

He nodded. "Thank you, ma'am."

"Oh, did you check your valuables with Maddie when you signed in? I can't be responsible if something goes missing."

"I've got nothing, ma'am," he said. A flash of anger washed across his face.

Had she offended him? "It's just that things get stolen from the rooms sometimes. No gun?"

He lowered his eyes. Perhaps he regretted his outburst. "No ma'am."

"Well, all right then." Annie left him alone and went to check the register. Arizona. He rode all the way from Arizona with no gun? An uncomfortable feeling rose in her throat, but she tried to dismiss it. Time to stop being suspicious. If things were to change around here, she had to change her thinking.

She'd better get those biscuits out of the oven. The hotel was full, and the school children would be over for lunch. A full day stretched out before her, and if she could keep Barney out of her head, it would be a good day.

~*~

She heard hammering before she even finished dressing. Annie always thought she was the first one up in Fort Stockton. She liked to throw open the front door and have her coffee on the veranda before starting the chores of the day. She finished dressing and looked out the kitchen window. She loved the early morning air, which in West Texas was generally always cool.

She missed the sound of the soldiers in the morning. It had been nearly twelve years since the Buffalo soldiers abandoned the fort grounds, just north of the hotel. She would hear them muster in the mornings and then go about their business. Their horses could surely kick up the dust.

The saloon across the street was stone cold quiet

so far. Some men in the town started their drinking early. Barney had been one of them.

Callie would be starting the laundry soon. It was a relief to have her busy, and not have to watch her sit in a hard, straight back chair with her hands folded, staring off in the distance.

Annie put the coffee on the top of the stove, knowing the scent would draw out the guests. She put bread in the oven that she'd set the night before, and started cracking eggs into a big cast iron skillet. While the eggs fried, she cut big slices of ham and tossed them in with the eggs. She retrieved her biscuit bowl from the shelf above the oven and started mixing her dough.

Frank walked into the kitchen. "Mrs. Riggs, I'm gonna need some tools. I found that old hammer on the ground behind the cabin as I was looking at all the damage. It's already broken."

"Of course, let me show you where you'll find some things. There's a woodpile out there where you can find some pieces to work with when you get to patching holes. Not like there's a place to buy wood. I'm sure you noticed there aren't many trees around here."

"Yes, ma'am. There's lots of mesquite in places."

"We don't use that for building, only for firewood. See what you can do with what we've got out back."

He nodded.

"I'll let you know when breakfast is ready. Take leave to eat whenever you get ready."

He nodded again.

The boy did not smile. She was used to cranky cowboys in the morning. Especially after they came dragging in from the saloon. But Frank Hankins had gone to bed early, no doubt tired from his ride. Maybe a good breakfast would cheer him up.

~*~

If only he could have been the one to kill Barney Riggs. He envied Beau Chadwick. Had Mrs. Riggs ordered the kill, as Charlie said? He'd spent his whole life planning to kill Barney Riggs, just as soon as he was old enough. Beau Chadwick beat him to it. Charlie's plan to help him get revenge made him nervous, but he forced himself to think about his poor mama, spending her nights in the Yuma saloon, thanks to Barney Riggs. She'd started going there after Pa got sent to prison. She left Frank in charge of baby Clyde. She'd come home after a weekend dead on her feet and almost incoherent. Frank thought in those early days that she was just sad about Pa. Frank would help her get to bed and then fix her something to eat. He'd want to tell her how hard it was while she was gone. That the baby wouldn't stop crying, and he'd burnt the biscuits again. They hadn't had nothing to eat but old bread while she was gone. Mama would sleep like the dead for two days, then she'd get up and try to help Frank with the baby. By the time the weekend rolled around again, she'd be getting ready to go to Yuma again. He dreamed about what Mama was like before Daddy went to prison. Long, brown hair, and laughing blue eyes. She cooked good things for them to eat, and even played with them some.

In Frank's mind, Annie Riggs was just as responsible for his family's misery as Barney Riggs. He'd kill her, but not before yanking her prosperous life right out from under her, the life his ma never got to have. Frank leaned over the wooden box of tools and tried to focus on his work for Mrs. Riggs. He could hear his mother's voice.

"Work is important, Frankie. A man that don't work is nothing in this world."

"Yes ma'am. That's what daddy says. I'm gonna help him fix the steps on the front porch this morning."

His mama did a funny thing with her lips when he said that. He must've said too much. She did like to say children should be seen and not heard. Maybe he said something wrong.

"Good boy, Frankie. Finish your breakfast, now, and get on out there."

Frankie ate up his beans and eggs as fast as a roadrunner slicing through the brush. He hadn't seen Pa this morning. Must be gettin' things ready to work on the porch.

Mama nursed baby Clyde while Frankie put his tin plate on the wooden counter by the water pump. He cranked the pump and washed his plate.

Mama was very proud of her silver. She said it was the only thing she brought with her from Kansas when she married Pa. She thought it was terrible to set silver forks and spoons beside tin plates on the table, but it was all she had.

"You be careful of that silver, now," she said it every

day.

"Yes, ma'am." He carefully dried the silver fork and put it in the velvet lined box on the fireplace mantel. "Pa said he's gonna buy you a set of china someday, Mama. It won't always look silly."

Mama made that face again. He'd better keep his mouth shut, that's what.

He climbed up to the loft and pulled on his trousers and buttoned up his shirt. It was getting too small for him. He found his cap under the rope bed and climbed back down. He hoped he could get some new clothes before he started school after the summer.

Just the word school sent a shiver down his spine. He just couldn't wait. He wanted to learn to read more than anything. He dreamed of reading Mama's Bible to the whole family in the evenings. He wanted to write down the stories that he made up in his head. As he backed down the ladder from the loft, he heard a knock at the door.

"Mrs. Jennings, where's John?" Sheriff Ferrell stood in the doorway. Mama shifted the baby up on her shoulder and stood up.

"He didn't come home, last night, Sheriff. You know," she began and then looked up at Frankie. She lowered her voice and coughed, "You know he likes to…spend time at the saloon."

"I'll just check out your story, if you don't mind." The sheriff walked around the cabin, He looked under Mama and Pa's rope bed, pushed Frank aside, and climbed up the ladder to the loft. He looked under Frank's bed.

"I'll check the outhouse," Sheriff Ferrell said.

"I'm tellin' you, Sheriff, he's not here." Mama backed

up to the sink with baby Clyde. She closed her eyes.

Directly, the sheriff barged back in the house. "I'll just wait here until he comes home."

"What's he done?" Mama began to cry.

Sheriff Ferrell looked at Frankie, and then back to Mama. He didn't say anything.

Mama never moved from the sink.

Frankie sat down at the table.

The sheriff stood by the window next to the front door, watching out Mama's muslin curtain.

A horse raced through the yard.

The sheriff dropped the curtain and stood behind the door.

Pa rushed in. "Elizabeth, I…" he began.

Sheriff Ferrell drew his gun and shoved it into Pa's back.

"'Elizabeth, I…'

"What, you no account. You've done yourself in for sure now."

Pa dropped a muslin bag he carried and threw both his hands in the air.

The sheriff kept the gun in Pa's back but squatted and picked up the bag. He pulled it open with his teeth and looked inside. Several wads of cash money tumbled onto the floor. "Yeah, Jennings. You've done it now. What's gonna happen to this little family of yours after this? I bet you didn't think of that, did you?" He nudged Pa toward the door and out on the porch, the bag in one hand and gun in the other.

Mama stayed straight as a board, leaning against the sink. Baby Clyde began to cry, but she didn't seem to notice.

Frankie tore his gaze from his sad Mama and tiptoed over the window. The sheriff kept his gun pointed at Pa as they stood on the porch. Two men rode into the yard. They climbed off their horses and rushed up on the porch, their guns drawn.

The sheriff took the saddle bags off Pa's horse. He pulled Pa's pistol from one of the bags and checked the bullet casing.

"Get up on your horse, and don't try to run. You'll get a taste of your own medicine if you do."

Three men held guns on his Pa. Frankie swallowed the urge to yell out, to cry. He watched Pa get on his horse and the four men rode away.

Mama slid to the floor and sobbed.

Frankie never saw his Pa again.

~*~

"Frank, would you ride over to the station and see if I have any mail on the freight wagon?" Annie thought he needed a break. He'd worked on Callie's cabin all day, and had said he'd go back out as soon as he ate.

"Yes, ma'am." He shoved a spoonful of beans into his mouth and stood up from the table at the same time.

"Whoa. Take your time. Sit down and eat." Mercy. If only her own boys were as quick to be helpful.

Frank sat down and finished his beans.

Annie took his plate and filled it with more beans, a piece of steak, and another biscuit.

"Thank you, Ma'am." He stabbed the piece of steak with his fork and tore off a bite.

"My goodness, Frank. Your mama never teach you to cut your food?" She took the forked piece of meat from his hand and cut it into pieces.

He flinched, and his lips pressed into a line. A flash of embarrassment, or maybe anger, widened his eyes and flushed his cheeks. His eyes narrowed. He swallowed hard. "We didn't have much steak growing up."

"I'm sorry, Frank. I didn't mean to insult you. I taught my own boys manners, but they don't always heed when they're working." Maybe his ma had passed, and he was still grieving. Something riled him up. She left the room so as not to embarrass him further.

A few hours later, he returned from the freight station with a letter.

"From Anabelle Clark in Atlanta!" she said. Oh, she'd thought about her best friend so many times. But when the cavalry left, so did Anabelle. Officer's wives shouldn't get too attached to town folk, the judge had warned her, but they were like two peas in a pod.

Dear Annie,

How I wish I could have been there for you when Barney died. I wanted to come, but traveling was out of the question at that time. Of course, it was in all the papers. I can't imagine what you've suffered. I was not surprised to read that you bought a hotel. Why, it wasn't even there when we were girls! How brave of you to carry on for your family.

I received your letter inquiring about the soldier in

Russell's unit, Lucius Smith. I've written letters to Russell's commanding officer and hope to provide some information soon.

I'm afraid I've had my own heartache. Russell was killed in the Arizona campaign. I wore the weeds for a year, but when I took them off, it still hurt. You know, don't you?

Yes, I do. Annie let the letter drop in her lap. Poor Belle. She'd loved Russell so. Annie let rare tears fall. She remembered how Russell teased them that Belle and Annie loved each other more than they did anyone else, him included. He was just about right, except that Belle Clark thought the sun rose and set on her tall, handsome husband. He was so busy, though, and Belle passed the time with Annie.

"Both our husbands cold in the grave. I can't believe it." Annie said aloud, and then wiped a tear from her eyes.

Our sons are both at West Point. Russell would be so pleased. I find that I have nothing but time on my hands and would like to come for a visit. I am so anxious to see you and make up for not being there when you needed me. I think just the sight of your face and a warm embrace will be the thing that pulls me out of the terrible darkness wherein I have wandered since the day Russell died.

You remember, I'm sure, how impetuous I was. Maybe a little of that is returning. I'm sending this letter off only a week before I plan to leave and head west. I hope the letter reaches you before I do. Don't go to any trouble but save me a bed in your hotel. I can't tell you how amazed I am that you are a businesswoman. It should come as no surprise to me or anyone else. You are the hardest working, strongest woman I know. No wallowing in self-pity for you.

I will see you in a few weeks. Until then, I am ever your Belle

Annie hugged the letter to her breast. Her heart raced with mixed emotions. To see Belle! What happy times they had. How wonderful it would be to have someone call her just Annie, not Mrs. Riggs or Mama.

Yet a tinge of anger wanted to surface. Annie had had no time to "wander in a terrible darkness". Her whole family had waited for her in the hotel dining room when she'd left Barney's bedside for the last time. Some of them depended on her for living. There had been only a brief few days of mourning, but then she'd played her grief out in work. She would overhear "strong Mrs. Riggs", "brave Mrs. Riggs", "he was a no account anyway" spoken behind her back. She had wanted to run screaming into the desert when Barney breathed his last. So many layers of disappointment and grief plagued her brain. But instead, she took control and did what she was supposed to do, what everyone expected.

Belle didn't have to work. She and Russell both came from wealthy families. She imagined Belle languishing on fine sheets in a silken black dress, wait staff rushing to meet her every need.

How unkind of me. Grief was grief, no matter how it manifests. She dismissed those bitter thoughts and let herself rejoice. Belle Clark was coming to Fort Stockton! She let her mind set to preparing a room for her. Maybe by her arrival she'd have information about Callie's husband.

Annie tucked the letter into her apron pocket and headed to the kitchen. She gathered up hot, fresh biscuits and arranged them in a wicker basket. She'd walk over to the school, give the new teacher the basket of biscuits for herself and the children, and then take a walk by the springs.

Just one hour to herself. It would be nice to let her mind roam to the time before husbands, back breaking work, and murder.

CHAPTER 6

Frank hammered away at the shingles on Callie's roof. He didn't mind being Mrs. Riggs's errand boy. It only served to make her trust him more. He'd even let her name his horse. He laughed at what she'd think if she knew he'd stolen it.

Biscuit whinnied as if he heard Frank's thoughts.

"You've gone soft on her, that's what. After this is over, I'll just bury you along with her."

Biscuit snorted and whickered.

He'd let himself get wrapped in the bubble that surrounded Annie Riggs, working for her, sharing meals, getting to know her family. He laughed to himself. He only had to make her trust him until he could convince her to give him the land that Barney promised Charlie. He wasn't sure how he'd do it yet. Charlie told him for now, just get in her good graces. Later, when his plan was accomplished, Charlie said Frank could shoot her the way Barney shot his father and have his revenge. They'd make it look as if one of the drunken cowboys at the saloon had shot her in an accident. He'd wait until everything was perfect and then rip the rug out from under the whole family. It would shake the whole town. His ma had never had the chance to do good to nobody, much less have any friends. His ma didn't have the strength to fix special meals for him, or even talk sweet. If Pa could have come home, Mama would have had a chance. He would have had a chance. Frank tossed the hammer onto the ground. Time to go for the mail. As he mounted Biscuit and headed for the station, his thoughts turned once again to his poor ma.

~*~

1887 in Yuma, Arizona

Frankie sat up in bed. What had awakened him so early? He rubbed sleep from his eyes and listened to the quiet house. He realized his ma wasn't crying. He'd grown so used to falling asleep with the sound of her sobs in his ears, and her hurt, as well as his, in his heart. He also awoke to her whimpering. Pa had gone to prison and would be there a long time.

She didn't make a sound this morning. Maybe his little brother was still asleep, and she didn't want to wake him. Had she finally started feeling better? Hope rose in his soul, and he threw on his shirt. He slid down the ladder from the loft, but as he landed on the cold floor, a sickening thought wracked his body. Was she dead?

He turned to find her at the stove, stirring a pot of meal. His stomach grumbled as he hadn't had a hot meal in days. Ma didn't smile or speak. She just slung a portion of meal into a plate and set it on the table. She sat down, motioned him to come and eat.

He joined her and took a spoonful of breakfast. No salt or sugar in this, but it still tasted good, and warmed his stomach.

"You want some, Ma?"

She shook her head, staring straight in front of her.

"Want me to make you a cup of coffee? I can do it. I've watched you lots of times." Was there any coffee?

She didn't answer, but just stared ahead. Finally she cleared her throat, and made eye contact with him. "I'm going to town. I got a job. There's nothing left to eat, and because of what your Pa's done, there's no help coming from anywhere." She looked away.

Frankie couldn't understand. His Pa was a thief, but his ma hadn't done anything. The anger that knocked at his heart pounded this time. He wouldn't get to start school, and he wasn't prepared when the news came. If Ma got a job, he'd have to take care of Clyde. He slammed the table with his fist, spoon still grasped.

He swallowed the words he was about to spout when he saw Ma's face. Her eyes filled with tears, and she bit her bottom lip. She was aware how badly he wanted to go to school, and it wasn't her fault.

"Don't you worry, Ma. I'll get a job, too. It's gonna be OK. And then when Pa gets home, it will be all right again."

Yes, he'd go to school when Pa came back home. He could wait until then. He'd have to. If he could just find someone to teach him to read in the meantime. Ma didn't know how. He wasn't sure, but he didn't think Pa could either.

Ma lay her head down on the table and began to cry.

Didn't she believe him? Everything would be all right.

Ma lifted her head, tears streaming down her cheeks. "You'll have to take care of the baby while I'm gone. I've got to get dressed. The man I'm working for is coming for me in his wagon." She rose slowly and walked toward her bed.

Frankie went outside so she could dress. He sat on the steps he'd repaired himself a few days after Pa was taken away. He'd learned to do many things by himself. He loved baby Clyde, but sometimes even Ma couldn't get him to stop crying. He'd do the best he could until Pa came home, and then he'd go to school.

A wagon rolled up the road, dust obscuring the driver. As the wagon pulled into the yard and the dust cleared, Frankie got a clear view of the man. His pock-marked face and thick eyebrows made him look like a villain on the cover of a dime novel. But he must be a nice man if Ma was working for him. The man didn't look at Frank or speak to him.

Ma came outside. She had on her best dress, the one with the calico skirt and lacy stuff around her neck. She must've pinched her cheeks because they were red. Her hair was brushed shiny.

"I'll try to bring you something home for supper," she said. "Don't be coming to town. Stay here and watch over the place and baby Clyde." She walked down the steps and climbed into the man's wagon without another word.

Frankie remembered when she used to hug him and kiss him. They drove away. She didn't even wave.

Frankie turned his mind to his chores. They'd already sold their cow and eaten all the chickens. The garden in winter was cold and hard. He went inside and washed up the dishes from breakfast and swept out the house. He sat down at the table with Ma's Bible and tried to make sense of the words.

The hours ticked away. Clyde was a good boy that day. They whiled the time wandering the yard. At dark, he lit a candle and put it in the window for Ma. There was no moon to speak of and he wanted to give her a little light to see to get in the house. He ate the leftover meal and fed some to the baby, washed up those dishes, put Clyde to bed, and sat at the table to wait.

He woke up the next morning, his head resting on the hard table, but she wasn't home. Ma never came home for two days.

~*~

Frank shook his head to clear the memory. He'd nearly arrived at the freight station. He'd pick up Mrs. Riggs's mail, his new weekly chore, and hightail it back. Charlie's strategy to help Frank seemed to be working. Each day she trusted him more put another nail in the coffin of the Riggs family. Could he really do it? Could he make her love him? Charlie said she'd be wanting a new husband. She was a site older than him, but still a handsome woman. She never cared a mite what people thought of her, he saw that right away. Annie Riggs did what she wanted in Fort Stockton. He admired and hated that at the same time because of the respect with which she was regarded. If his ma had only had a chance.

The freight wagons had beaten him to the station. The stage had come and gone. A woman in a blue silk dress and a hat too ornate for the West Texas wind and dust stood next to a buckboard that had arrived with the wagons. Her bags surrounded her on the ground. Probably a guest for the hotel. He'd offer to take her there.

Frank dismounted and walked toward the wagonmaster, "Any mail for the hotel?"

Before the driver could answer, the woman in silk stepped toward him. "Are you from the hotel? Are you here to take me there? I hope so. I'm so ragged out I don't think I could walk there, not with all these bags."

Frank removed his hat. "I can lead you there, Ma'am. If you can ride my horse, I'll carry your bags and take you to the Riggs Hotel."

"Oh, you dear man. I'd be ever so grateful." She heaved a heavy sigh of relief.

"Here's the mail, Hankins." The driver passed down a small bundle.

He nodded his thanks and turned to the woman. "Are you ready to go now?"

"Surely you jest. If I don't get there and rest in a comfortable bed within the next hour, I'm sure I'll perish." She dabbed at her neck with a lace handkerchief.

Frank helped her up on the horse. She arranged herself side-saddle. He started to pick up her bags.

"No, Lem can carry them." She waved a dismissive hand toward the buckboard.

A tall black man stepped down. He picked up the woman's bags.

The driver threw another bag to the ground.

Lem picked that one up too. He wore a kepi hat.

"I let him ride with me because his brother was in

my husband's unit."

Frank flinched at her condescending explanation, and then nodded to Lem with a smirk.

She pulled an ornate contraption from a pearl festooned bag and began to fan herself.

Frank took Biscuit's reins and led him toward the hotel. They walked along without a word.

Lem followed behind.

Half an hour later they approached the hotel.

Annie was sitting on the veranda with Callie having a cup of tea. "Belle!" Annie cried. She stood and bounded down the steps.

"Lucius!" Callie cried, rising from her chair, her teacup crashing to bits on the veranda. "Lucius, I knew you'd come back!" Callie rushed down the steps. She threw her arms around Lem. "I knew you'd come for me. Didn't I tell you Mrs. Annie? My Lucius has come for his Callie."

Annie's jaw dropped. Belle found Callie's Lucius? Unbelievable.

Lem put down the bags and gently pulled her away. He took both her hands in his. "Mrs. Caledonia Smith. I'm Lem, Lucius's brother."

"Oh, don't be jokin' me now. You're my Lucius. See, I told you Mrs. Annie. I told you he'd come back to me."

"Well, no, Callie, wait a minute." Annie stepped toward her. Poor Callie. Would this push her over the edge?

Belle held out her arms for Frank to help her down.

Annie embraced her as soon as she was on the ground. "Let's get you inside. You must be exhausted," Annie said.

"More tired than I've ever been in my life, I think. I can scarcely put two thoughts together." Belle folded her fan and put it in her bag.

Annie slid her arm around her dear friend's waist and helped her toward the stairs. Lem did look very much like his older brother, and seemed about the same age as Lucius when he'd left seventeen years earlier, so to Callie he must be Lucius.

"Let's all go in and let our guests freshen up. Callie, you can help me get a meal on the table."

"Yes, Mrs. Annie." Callie slid her arm through Lem's. Her eyes beamed and brimmed with tears.

Lem looked at Annie for answers. Annie tried not to think about how that would play out. Maybe Lem could make her understand.

"I got me a cabin out back, Lucius, all fixed up real nice," Callie said. She put her arms around Lem's waist and hugged him. She let him go and went into the kitchen.

Annie showed Belle to her room.

"The day I mailed the letter telling you I was coming, I received word about Lucius. He did perish in the Arizona campaign, same as Russell. The colonel also informed me that his brother Lem lived right there in Atlanta! I convinced him to come with me and collect his sister-in-law." Belle took off her hat as she spoke. "I've got to get out of this dress."

"Of course, dear. I'll bring you some refreshment

and you can rest. We'll visit this evening. I'm so glad you're here." Annie gave Belle another hug, and then returned to the dining room and pulled Lem aside. "I'm sorry, Mr. Smith. I didn't know you were coming. I'm afraid that Callie lost a baby in childbirth the same day Lucius rode out with the cavalry. The grief of that and Lucius' absence caused her to be a bit, well, touched. She's been searching for Lucius every day since, and I'm afraid you look just like him, well, the way he looked years ago. I don't know how we'll make her understand."

Lem sat in a chair. "Mrs. Clark told me that Lucius had left a wife. We never got no letters from him. I was just a boy, but I know my big brother. If he told her he'd come back for her, he meant to. I'm sorry to hear they lost a child."

"It was a boy. Lived one night. Callie named him Lemuel, said that's what Lucius had wanted."

Lem's face fell, and he dropped his head into his hands. "I'll try to make her understand."

Frank hovered nearby.

Annie breathed a sigh of thanks to have someone just waiting to help. She wasn't used to that. "Frank, show Lem where he can get washed up for supper. You won't mind sharing your room with him tonight, will you?"

"That's fine, Mrs. Riggs. Come on, Lem."

Lem followed Frank out of the dining room into the courtyard.

Callie was in the kitchen. She sliced ham and placed the pieces neatly on a plate. She sang a tune that

Annie was very familiar with. "Hard times, hard times come again no more."

Annie winced at Callie beatific expression.

"I told you, Mrs. Annie. And he's come. My Lucius has come."

~*~

Frank and Lem walked across the courtyard toward Frank's room.

One of the cowboys staying at the hotel walked outside his room. "That darkie ain't staying here is he?"

Every muscle in Frank's body stiffened. "What's it to you?"

"Mrs. Riggs 'llow a man like that in her hotel?" He leaned up against the roof pole.

"Again, what's it to you?"

The cowboy stepped toward Frank and sneered, nose to nose.

"That's OK, Mr. Frank. I don't want no trouble." Lem turned to leave.

"No trouble here, Lem. You go on inside my room."

"So you gonna let that man sleep in your bed? What kind of trash are you?" The cowboy laughed.

Frank let the word "trash" get stuck in his craw. The only way he could get it out was to double up his fist and lay it firmly on that cowboy's face. The cowboy stumbled back and fell. He jumped up and met Frank with his own fists. The two went at it all over the courtyard.

Annie rushed out. "Stop it, stop it now, I say."

Frank got up off the dirt and bent, grabbing his knees to catch his breath.

The other man rolled on the ground, holding his face.

"Seems this cowboy here has a problem with Lem staying at your hotel," Frank said, between breaths.

"I see." Annie walked over to the cowboy on the ground, grabbed his shirt just under his neck, and yanked him to his feet.

Frank went wide-eyed at her strength.

"Get your stuff and get out." Annie put her fists on her hips.

"Don't want to stay here anyway, not with that darkie in the bed just down the row." he said through muffled, swollen lips.

After he left, Frank approached Annie in the kitchen. "I'm real sorry, ma'am. I know you don't cotton to fightin'. The jerk just got on my nerves."

"I would have done the same thing," Annie said, not turning from her work.

Frank believed she would.

CHAPTER 7

Frank finished replacing floorboards in Miss Callie's cabin. Mrs. Riggs had sent her and Lem in the wagon for a ride so he could finish up inside. Maybe Lem could make Miss Callie understand about her poor dead husband. Frank put away the tools and sat on the back porch of the hotel to cool off.

Gene walked out onto the back porch with a tart in each hand.

"Mama wants to know if you want a peach tart. Cuz if you don't, I will eat them both." The little fellow took a bite out of one of the tarts and sat down on the bench next to Frank.

Irritation rose in Frank, constricting his throat. He coughed it away and found his voice. The tow-headed boy held the tart toward him, but Frank waved it away. "What are you so dressed up for, Buster Brown?"

"I ain't Buster, my name's Gene. We're goin' to church." He made quick work of the first tart, and then started on the second one.

Typical. Navy sailor suit with a wide starched collar, walking around with benefits Frank never got. He only hoped that Clyde had been afforded such luxuries.

"Mama makes good peach tarts, but you don't know that cuz you wouldn't eat one. You wanna go to church with us?"

"Did your Ma tell you to ask me that?"

"Yeah, Mr. Frank, it's only down the road to St. Joseph's."

"I'll pass, but thanks, just the same. How come I don't see much of you?"

"I stay at Mrs. Piña's while my ma works."

The back door opened, and Mrs. Riggs walked outside. "Time to go Gene, come in and wash your hands. Did you offer Frank a treat?"

"He didn't want it, so I ate it," he said, slipping behind his mother into the hotel.

Mrs. Riggs shook her head. "That boy loves his desserts. I dare say he didn't offer with enough enthusiasm, likely."

She wore a hat with a large feather, and her gown matched the fabric in her hat. His ma wore feathers, but somehow, they looked different on Mrs. Riggs. No, it was the dress that was different. Mrs. Riggs's dress had more to it, covered up more. He felt the anger rise and swallowed hard. "I'm not hungry, thanks anyway." He wished she'd leave so he could get to his room.

"All right. I'll be out for an hour or so. Maddie is working the desk."

"Yes ma'am."

Gene appeared in the screen door behind her. "Maddie washed my hands, Ma, let's go."

Mrs. Riggs stared at Frank as though she wanted

to speak but turned and left.

Frank barely got to his room before the memory rolled over him. He couldn't stop it.

~*~

1887 in Yuma

Frankie awoke to knocking on the front door. He sat up in bed and rubbed the sleep from his eyes. He leaned over the loft and watched Ma pull Baby Clyde off from nursing.

She straightened her blouse and hugged the baby close to her. The knocking became more persistent.

"Mrs. Jennings, we've come this morning, just as we agreed," a man called from the front porch.

Mama buried her nose in Clyde's soft neck.

Frankie could hear her crying. A sick dread twisted his empty stomach.

"I've brought my wife, Mrs. Jennings," he called. "We'll take care of the baby, just as you agreed. Please open the door."

"No!" Frankie shouted. He hurried down the ladder in his night shirt. He fell off the last step, twisting his ankle. It hurt too much to stand on it when he tried, so he crawled over to the front door. He spread his arms across the width of it, his back pressed against it.

"No, Ma. I can take care of Baby Clyde. I've been doing it just fine, you said so yourself. Please don't let them take him, Ma, please." Tears ran down his cheeks and into his nose, but he'd not take his arms away from the door for anything.

"Move, Frankie. It's for the best. I can't give him what

he needs. It's just for a time, until things get better. It's the travelin' preacher and his wife; they'll take good care of him." She stood and stepped toward the door. "Move, Frankie."

Frankie stood to his full height, his ankle throbbing. "I don't want to defy you, Ma, but I can't let this happen. Please give me a chance to take care of him." The door edged open behind him. Ma took his arm and pulled him out of the way. Baby Clyde started crying. The preacher pushed his way in the door, his wife following.

Ma handed the baby to the preacher's wife.

Clyde began to scream and put his little arms out to Frankie.

"Helga, take the baby out to the wagon," the preacher said.

"No, no you don't either," Frankie yelled and limped toward the baby.

The preacher's wiry arms restrained him, and Frankie tried to wrestle him to the ground.

"Stop, Frankie," Ma said, tears pooling in her eyes. She stepped over to him. "Unhand my boy, Preacher," Ma said.

Frankie fell into her arms. "Ma, don't let them take him, please." He looked into her eyes. A glimmer of hope pierced the stone in his stomach as Ma looked toward the door.

"Remember, Mrs. Jennings, that a woman of your, um, employment, has no business taking care of a baby. The wife and I can give Clyde all the things he needs, including a proper upbringing and education. If your situation changes, he can come back home."

"You won't never bring him back. You'll love him too and not ever give him back," Frankie cried. "Ma?"

Ma's tears flowed as she looked away from the front door. "Get out. Take him and get out."

She held Frankie tight as the preacher wasted no time running out the door. As it slammed behind him, she slipped to the floor, letting go of Frank.

Frankie bolted. He nearly yanked the door off its hinges as he limped out as fast as he could. "Stop!"

The preacher's horses had already pulled the wagon out of the gate. The dust kicked up and stung his eyes, but he tried to follow anyway. "Clyde," Frankie cried. He couldn't reach them, but he could hear his baby brother crying. Frankie tried to get a last glimpse of his face, but it was too late.

How could she do that? How could she send him away? His first thought was to hide in the barn and cry. Then he just wanted to yell at Ma. His hurt and anger propelled him back into the house. He took a deep breath to start in on her.

She lay in a heap on the floor and wailed.

It jangled his nerves. Of course, it hurt her as much as it did him, but he still couldn't understand. He knelt beside her. "Ma, why? I can take care of him, you know I can."

She sat up, and through her sobs she said, "You have to get a job, Frankie. We're not making it. You have to go into town and find a job. You won't be here to take care of him. We'll get him back, I promise."

"But Ma, Pa will be home soon and everything will be all right again. Please, Ma, stop them from taking him."

She sat up and held her stomach with both hands, her eyes swollen and red. "Your Pa ain't never coming home, Frankie. He done been kilt by a man named Barney Riggs."

Frankie limped out the door and let it slam. He made his

way down the road until the dust stung his eyes and filled his throat. He watched the cloud of dirt that encircled the preacher's wagon get farther and farther away. Frankie turned and struggled around to the back of the barn and punched the wall until his hand hurt.

Pa kilt? Would he ever see baby Clyde again? His stomach rose to his throat. He kicked his one good foot into the barn, and threw himself on the ground. The name Barney Riggs seared itself into his soul.

A week later, after he got over being mad at his ma, Frank decided to waste no more time and started out to look for a job. He wanted to help Ma, and he needed something to keep his mind off Clyde. Ma reminded him of a locust shell, completely empty, stuck, and not able to move. She missed a few days of work, and Frank hoped she wouldn't go back. But the saloon owner came out one afternoon and picked her up.

Before this day, Frank went to sleep every night dreaming of going to school and reading Ma's Bible. Now, he would cover his head with the blanket Ma made him and think about how to get big enough and brave enough to find Clyde and bring him home. Find Clyde and kill Barney Riggs.

After Ma left for work one morning, Frankie walked to town. Maybe he could find out when the preacher would be back through. Surely Ma could get Clyde back if both she and Frank brought in money.

He walked by the saloon and heard a familiar laugh, kind of like the way Ma used to laugh before Pa left. The sound made his heart tingle, and he couldn't resist taking a peek inside the swinging doors.

The sound came from a frilly lady sitting on a fat cowboy's lap. Her legs were uncovered, and he felt his face flush. She had on a lacy skirt and just her petticoat on top and a big feather in her hair. The cowboy put his swollen, dirty hand on the lady's leg. She laughed, and as his eyes focused on her face, he realized it was Ma. His heart pounded as he burst into the saloon.

"You get your hands off my Ma!" he yelled. He grabbed Ma and tried to pull her from the strange man's lap. He pushed the man out of his chair and jumped on him, beating him in the face with both hands. The man's nose spouted blood.

"Frankie! Stop it! You run home now, you hear?" Ma grabbed his shirt and pulled him off the fuming, bloody cowboy. "Get home!"

"Come with me, Ma. This ain't no place for you. What would Pa think?"

The men in the saloon erupted in laughter.

Frankie took his Ma by the hand and tried to pull her to the door.

Another man with an apron on came around from behind the bar. "Unhand her, boy. She can't leave now. She's got too much work to do. Didn't you know what your mama does for a living?"

Laughter arose again, and the men raised their glasses to his Ma.

She ignored them, put her hands on Frankie's shoulders, and spoke a little softer, "Get home now."

The man on the floor wiped his nose. "Kid just found out he's trash, just like his mama," he said, laughing as he shoved a bloody handkerchief into his pocket.

Frankie ran outside. He ran through town blindly. He tripped and landed face down in the dirt. His nose bled. He sat up and walked to the back of the livery and then crouched beside a pile of hay. He had to think of a way to get Ma out of that place. "Trash." The word got louder and louder in his head. He cried until he fell asleep.

He awoke to find a young black girl dabbing a cloth to his nose. "What on earth happened to you, boy?"

Frankie didn't respond.

"You the boy that ran outta the saloon? Found out your mama is a working girl? Tsk, tsk," she said shaking her head. She took off her shawl and wrapped it around his shoulders. "You come with me, now. I'll get you something to eat." She led him down the street to a small shack beside the post office. "I'm the laundress for this part of town, me and my mama."

Laundry! A sudden hope lifted his spirits. His ma could do laundry instead of working in that awful place. "Do you think you could give my Ma a job?"

"She ain't gonna come in here when she's making a sight more money where she is. Now don't you be too hard on her. Ain't much a woman can do 'round here when she been abandoned."

How did this girl know so much about it?

She cleaned him up some more, and then brought him a piece of cornbread.

Frankie ate it in two bites.

"Law! You must be starving'" She brought him another piece.

Frankie made quick work of again.

"Now you better get home befo' it gets dark. If'n you

ever need anything, you come on back and see Sissy. I can usually come up with some cornbread and maybe some beans."

"Do you know when the travelin' preacher comes through here? He took my baby brother the last time. I aim to get him back."

Sissy's eyes lowered, and she sniffed. "Now that's mighty noble of you. If'n I hear of him comin' I'll get word to you."

"Thank you, ma'am."

She giggled. "Oh, go on with you now, calling me ma'am. Ain't nobody called me ma'am unless they was jokin'." She led him to the door.

Frankie didn't want to leave. He felt safe and cared for the way it used to be when Ma and Pa were both at home. He knew now why his ma came home so tired, and sometimes never came home at all.

"Wait, just a minute," Sissy said. She went to her cupboard and pulled a piece of paper out. She wrapped another piece of cornbread up in the paper and slipped it into Frankie's coat pocket. "For the road," she said.

He planned to give it to his ma when she came home.

"Now, you run on over to the carpenter's shop. I think they're lookin' for an errand boy."

~*~

Annie kept the sideboard stocked with ham, beans, and biscuits. Depending on what she could get, she also made pies. Her famous peach cobbler delighted the locals and visitors alike. But more often than not, the guests just poured syrup on their biscuits. Not tonight, though.

She set the table for Belle, Lem, Callie, Frank, and herself. She bit her bottom lip at the thought of what fine dishes Belle might be used to, but she put out her Blue Willow china anyway. She'd baked two chickens, boiled potatoes with salt, pepper, and butter, and cooked up the last of the green beans. She made a buttermilk pie and uncorked the one bottle of wine she had left. She really needed to restock, but things were hard to come by. Kettler's store carried most necessities, but luxuries were hit and miss between supply wagon days.

She went for Belle, and then knocked on Frank's door. "Time for supper. I'd like you to join us and help me make my new guests comfortable." It might go a ways to makin' that boy smile a bit, too.

"Yes, ma'am."

The five sat around the table. Callie couldn't take her eyes off Lem.

The guests dove into that meal.

Well, all but Belle, who picked at the plate with her pinky finger extended.

Annie frowned and wondered how Belle would enjoy her visit if she couldn't eat. Annie would have to try to get an idea of what she could cook for her.

After the meal, they went into the parlor.

Annie served coffee, and then she played the piano.

"Play that pathetic piece you used to play that made everyone cry," Belle said. "What was it?"

"We used to trio with Russell on 'Tis But a Little Faded Flower.' I think I still have the sheet music." Annie slid off the piano bench so she could open it. She rummaged through a large selection of sheet music and found the one she wanted. She sat down and played the introduction.

Belle stood and joined her at the piano.

Annie's alto perfectly accompanied Belle's soprano melody.

This but a little faded flower,
But oh, how fondly dear!
'Twill bring me back one golden hour,
Through many a weary year.
I may not to the world impart
The secret of its power,
But treasured in my inmost heart,
I keep my faded flower.
Where is the heart that doth not keep,
Within its inmost core,
Some fond remembrance, hidden deep,
Of days that are no more?
Who hath not saved some trifling thing
More prized than jewels rare--
A faded flower, a broken ring,
A tress of golden hair?

Belle barely finished that last phrase before bursting into tears. "I miss Russell's bass," she cried.

Annie stood and embraced her.

Callie brought in more coffee, and the two old friends reminisced for an hour, while Frank sat silent.

Lem helped Callie with the dishes, and then they

joined the party.

"I'd like to take Miss Callie for a walk, if you don't mind, Mrs. Riggs." Lem stood, his hat in his hand.

Callie grinned from ear to ear.

"Of course, I'm sure you have many things to talk about. Callie, show Lem your cabin since it's all fixed up."

"Lucius," she said, correcting Annie. "Mr. Frank fixed it up real nice, Lucius. You'll like it."

Lem took Callie by the hand, and they walked out the front door.

"I hope he can make her understand. I may have done wrong trying to find out about Lucius. If she can shake off the cloud in her head and realize that he's dead, she might improve. But what do I know of mental issues? Regardless, Lucius's people are her people now. You think Lem will take her home with him?" Annie asked.

"I don't know," Belle said. "He told me on the trip here that he has a wife and children of his own."

"Wonder why he came all this way, then," Annie said.

"He only said that he needed to see about Lucius's wife. Maybe he could help her in some way. He didn't say anything about taking her back to Atlanta."

Annie prayed silently. A realization that Lucius was never coming back might push Callie over the edge to complete mental breakdown. She regretted sticking her nose into matters. Still, Callie deserved a better life than just breaking her back and ruining her hands doing laundry. It broke Annie's heart to watch her stare toward the north, waiting for a man who was never coming back. If Lem didn't take her to Atlanta, Annie determined to continue to care for Callie, no matter what. She'd hire someone else to do laundry and train Callie to do something else. Maybe a change would help her.

After everyone had gone to bed, Annie rocked in her rocking chair, nursing a cup of warm milk. Lem and Callie had never returned to the hotel. She got up to look out the kitchen window at Callie's cabin.

They were sitting on the bench outside the cabin door. Lem held her hand and was arduously speaking to her. Annie prayed.

Directly, the awful wailing of complete desperation rose over the south end of Fort Stockton. Annie reached for her throat and squeezed her eyes shut. She sank onto the floor, knowing the pain that Callie was just stabbed with, a pain that Annie had never had the chance to express. The cry ceased, and Annie rose to venture a look out the kitchen window.

Callie had collapsed into Lem's arms, and her shoulders shook.

Thank God for a kind man who would hold her tight and grieve with her. Annie wondered what kind of mental state Callie would be in when the crying stopped. It would be a long night.

In the wee hours of the morning, Lem came into the hotel.

Annie was still rocking in the parlor.

"Mrs. Riggs, Callie has gone to sleep. I put her in her bed, but I don't think it's right for me to stay in the cabin with her. I'm not sure if she'll remember the truth when she wakes up." He looked as though he'd been run over by a herd of sheep.

"Of course, I'll stay with her. You try and get some sleep." Annie retrieved a shawl from her room and wrapped it around her shoulders. She pumped some water into a jar and grabbed a box of tea from the cabinet.

Lem stood in the door, his hat in his hands.

"Do you think she understands?" Annie asked.

"It's hard to tell, but when I showed her a picture of my wife and children, she came undone. I don't know if she thinks Lucius married someone else, or if she understood that I am his brother with my own family, and that Lucius isn't coming back. Something tore her heart to pieces, though." He slumped against the door frame with a heavy sigh. He straightened and followed Annie out to the cabin. He sat on the bench as she went inside. He was still sitting there when she came out as the sun came up.

"She's still asleep."

"Good, Mrs. Riggs, thank you so much."

"You should go to your room and get some sleep. I'll let you know if she wakes up. I'm sure you didn't sleep much on the trip, and you didn't sleep all night."

"You're right about that. Much obliged," he said, and went inside the hotel.

Whether Callie Smith believed Lucius was dead, or that he'd betrayed her, things would be different when she awoke.

CHAPTER 8

Annie had to get breakfast for her guests, no matter what had happened during the night. She popped biscuits in the oven and then started frying eggs.

Frank entered the kitchen.

"You didn't seem to know any of the songs we were playing and singing last night, Frank."

"I didn't have much music growing up, Mrs. Riggs."

"I see. Well, we'll have to remedy that. I have something you might enjoy." She led him to the parlor and opened the lid of a shining wooden box. She took a set of keys from her apron pocket and unlocked a cabinet door at the bottom of the tall piece of furniture, retrieved a giant horn, and attached it to the base.

"A phonograph!" Frank walked closer. "I saw this last night and wondered if it worked."

"I keep it locked because I don't want it broken by a drunken guest. As hard as I try to enforce the rules, they still come in here after drinking at the saloon. The parts are hard to come by, and so are the discs. But let me show you how to use it, and you can get caught up on at least a few pieces of music. She put a disc on the machine and, cranked it up. She positioned the needle, and the music began.

"I've got to finish breakfast; you just enjoy yourself for a few minutes."

A half hour later Frank came into the kitchen and stood right next to Annie at the stove. "I enjoyed that, Mrs. Riggs. I have to admit, though, I'd rather hear you play piano."

"Well, thank you. Let me slip past you and go in the parlor and put the phonograph away," Annie said. *Why'd he stand so close? Afraid someone would hear him say he liked the music?*

"I've already done it, Ma'am. Want me to lock it? You can go on about your business," he said.

"Thank you, yes." She handed him the keys. Well, finally a little life showing in that boy. Music will do it every time.

Frank took the keys, but held on to her hand, never taking his eyes from her. He opened his mouth slightly, as if to speak.

Standing so close to her, she realized just how tall he was. She looked up into his eyes. Annie hadn't noticed just how deep blue his eyes were, very much like Barney's. The thought of her dead husband caused her to blink. She stepped back in bewilderment. *Now just what is on this boy's mind?*

He stepped away and headed to the parlor.

Surely he just intended to express gratitude. The boy was a mystery, that was for sure and certain.

He returned with the keys. "I'll go do my chores, now."

"Have you given any thought to when you might

head on to San Angelo?" Annie asked.

"I should have already left, but I've just enjoyed being here way too much."

"Well, no rush, we've all gotten used to you." Yes, the young man was just grateful.

Frank's face grew red, and he turned away. She must have embarrassed him. She had the feeling his life in Arizona had been unusually hard. He was reluctant to talk about his family, but he seemed so intense about certain things.

He walked out of the kitchen, just as Belle came in. She looked as if she'd slept for weeks; her face had more color, and her eyes shone, a little too bright. Probably just the after effects of the long ride. Annie hoped she could eat the simple breakfast fare. She hadn't had time to come up with something fancy for Belle. She wouldn't know what to fix differently anyway.

Annie related to Belle the events of the night.

"I'm perfectly horrified. Poor little dear. If she goes completely mad, you'll have quite a problem on your hands," Belle said.

Annie needed something a little more encouraging than that, but she had to admit to herself that Belle's insensitive comment was true. There was no hospital near, and Annie already had her hands full. Callie, even in her reduced state of mind, had been helpful. She had gotten in the habit of bringing Annie a cup of tea at day's end. She didn't talk much, but they had developed camaraderie of sorts. It didn't matter, Annie would take care of Callie, no matter what. "Breakfast is on the sideboard, Belle, whenever you're ready. I need to run an errand; I won't be long. Take your food to your room if you like."

Belle yawned and nodded.

Annie took a fresh batch of biscuits out of the oven and put them on a plate on the sideboard, then headed out the front door for a trip to Kettler's. Mr. Kettler liked to swap biscuits for a few supplies. She walked down the hill.

Frank slipped into the Grey Mule across the street.

She'd seen that Frank tended to go in the saloon in the daytime when there were no customers. Annie thought that odd. Maybe he was doing work for Charlie Simmons as well. She didn't blame him for wanting to work, but she knew Charlie probably filled his head with poison. Frank didn't act as if he'd been influenced by Charlie, though. No one had ever hated her in her life that she knew about, except Charlie Simmons. Barney had mentioned to her that he'd promised Charlie a couple of acres on that tract out east of town. If he'd ever stop spewing hatred at her, she'd let him know. It would be a relief if he'd pack up and move out to those few acres and leave her alone.

~*~

"So, looks as though you're getting' in her good graces. She's treating you like a member of the family," Charlie said. He wiped out shot glasses with a dirty rag.

"That's just what I want. Barney Riggs ruined any

chance of our family recovering from the mess my Pa made. I promised myself I'd make sure his family pays for it." The words he said fit his mission but he had a hard time making them true in his heart. He downed a shot of whiskey. He'd dang sure make it true.

Chapter 9

Annie returned from Kettler's to find Chef Francoise Fournier sitting on the porch. Was it really necessary for him to wear his toque all over town? He wanted everyone to know he was the chef, the *French* chef of the Stockton Hotel across town. What could he possibly want?

She extended her hand for a shake. "Hello, Mr. Fournier, how nice of you to visit," she said.

"Thank you, Mrs. Riggs," he said. He swooped off his toque, bowed low, and then kissed her hand. When he finally up-righted himself, he gave her a suspicious grin.

"Can I get you some coffee?" she asked, resisting the urge to wipe her hand off on her apron.

"I would like to sample your famous biscuits. The Stockton serves the finest cuisine available in this god-forsaken place, and yet all I hear is "you have to try Mrs. Riggs's biscuits."

She'd never been to France, so she could not compare, but god-forsaken? Not her beloved Fort Stockton.

"I take exception to your description of my home. Obviously you haven't found its beauty to your liking." She stopped just in the kitchen doorway and crossed her arms.

He replaced his toque. "And what beauty would that be, Mrs. Riggs? Heat, prickly plants, wind?"

"Sunsets, and cool evenings to watch those sunsets, water, fruit trees, artistic cloud horizons painted by God himself, fire and charcoal sunrises," she began.

"Ah, I had not heard that you were so, um, poetic. I do concede that the fruit gives me something to work with in the dessert area, but the rest has not caught my fancy. Perhaps I'll come and watch a sunset with you sometime. Now, madam, the biscuits?"

"Oh, certainly, please, sit here in the dining room. The biscuits are an old family recipe. There's a fresh batch here on the breakfast board." He sat down at the table, his wide-eyed eagerness reminding her of Gene when he waited for peach cobbler after supper. She brought out a plate, napkin, saucer of butter, and a fork from the kitchen. The biscuits were done to a turn, still warm. She slathered fresh butter between two halves, set the plate before him and stood back.

"Ah, thank you, madam," he said.

He took great care in looking the biscuit over. He brought a half to his nose and sniffed. His eyes blinked for a few seconds, but then returned to normal as if he didn't want her to know he was in heaven, and then took a bite. He chewed a bit, and then it mashed it around on his tongue. "Simple ingredients, but there is something I cannot detect. Pray, what is the thing I am missing?" He took another bite and chewed in earnest this time.

"It's a family recipe and not available to the public." She didn't thank him because he didn't compliment the taste.

"I see. Can you be persuaded to sell the recipe to me exclusively?" He stood, his napkin falling to the floor.

"No, I don't think so, but thanks just the same," she said, clearing his dishes.

"Ah, Mrs. Riggs. Surely you would enjoy some cash to do some," he looked around and screwed up his nose, "much needed renovations." He waved his arms around as though dismissing her beloved hotel.

"Be that as it may, I am not interested in selling my recipe."

Chef Fournier sniffed and crossed his arms.

He looked at her as though she had three heads. She couldn't help but laugh. "Why are you so intent on my recipe? I'm sure your biscuits are," she coughed slightly, "adequate."

He raised his head and gave a slight gasp, as though he remembered something. "Every business owner in town has been contacted for a meeting at the Stockton to discuss the possibility of backing the railroad. My employer wants to put on a meal that will please them and put them in an agreeable mood. I believe he seeks to make deals with the railroad about housing their foremen when the project goes through."

Not every business owner. She was tempted to be angry at having been left out. But to have the trains come through Fort Stockton would be a dream come true. It was the key to changing the West from violence to a peaceable place to raise a child.

"Perhaps you will agree to cook the biscuits for the meeting next month. I will see that you and your hotel receive full credit. It can only help your enterprise. Please, I cannot return to the hotel empty handed." He tried to reach for her hand, but she crossed her arms.

Although she was not one to pass up an opportunity to augment her assets, this compromise she would not make. The Stockton Hotel might secure special arrangements with the Orient Line, but their guests would still have to come to her establishment if they wanted the best biscuits.

"I'm not interested. Good day, Chef Fournier," she said, giving him a final nod of her head.

"Ach! Well, it's only biscuits, my dear woman. You are not the only one with skills. I sought only to provide a favorite of this community, with full credit to the formidable Mrs. Riggs. I'm reminded, though, that I also provide many foods that you wouldn't begin to know anything about cooking. Good day, madam." He left in a huff, slamming the door behind him.

Annie sat down at the dining room table and laid her head on her arms. She dissolved into a fit of laughter that rang out through the hotel. What a strange man. It was only biscuits.

Frank came into the room. "Well, I was about to deck him. How disrespectful. Are you all right?"

"More than all right. What nonsense."

"So, you have a secret recipe, that's nice," Frank said.

"No, not really. But some years past a rumor was

started that I had a secret recipe. I don't see any reason to disappoint. People enjoy them because they think there is something special about them. It's only the same recipe anyone else uses, most likely. It's an illusion."

"I don't know, Mrs. Riggs. I think your biscuits are taller than any I've ever had."

"Well, I can't imagine what makes them different than anyone else's biscuits. Maybe it's the cream of tartar. It's not readily available everywhere. But it's no secret, everyone makes their biscuits with it."

"Ah, so you order it special."

"Yes. I get nervous when I'm about to run out and the shipment is still weeks out. Don't want to disappoint folks."

Frank crossed his arms, sniffed, and mimicked Chef Fournier.

Annie broke into laughter again.

She didn't know what had made that boy so solemn when he first hit town, but she was delighted that he seemed to be warming up to life in Fort Stockton.

"Is there anything you'd like me to do today, Mrs. Riggs?"

"Actually, I was wondering if you would drive me to the freight station. I want to deliver some food samples to the station master's wife. She's thinking of offering food to the passengers who are only stopping for a bit and then traveling on. She'd want me to deliver it every day. I don't have time for that but I can probably get someone to do it."

Frank brought the buggy around to the front of the hotel as Annie descended the steps. Belle stood on the street corner talking to Chef Fournier. It hadn't occurred to her that he might give her ideas of what to cook for Belle. Now he probably wouldn't speak to her. *I should have been nicer to him*. What if Belle went to the Stockton Hotel to eat? She'd try not to let it bother her. It would be good for Belle to make friends. Maybe she'd stay a good long while.

Two hours later Annie and Frank returned to the hotel to find Belle in a flush of excitement.

"I met your *darling* Chef Fournier, and he's invited me to confer with him on the menu at the Stockton Hotel. He wants to know all the latest cuisine that the chefs are preparing in Atlanta. I finally feel useful around here."

"I see," Annie said. It bothered her more than she thought it would. Why hadn't Belle offered some input into the menu at the Riggs? Useful? Belle could make herself useful helping Annie in the kitchen or making her own bed, for that matter. Annie had waited on her hand and foot since she'd arrived, and that on top of her regular duties.

No use getting her back up about it. She'd realized soon enough that although they'd been close friends as girls, Belle and Annie separated into two different worlds. Belle's refined life of wealth and privilege distanced itself from Annie's life of hard work and violence as far as the east was from the west. Time and experience made it difficult for the women to fall into their old chummy routine. She expected Belle would likely return to Atlanta soon. At least they shared memories of their youth, and the sorrow of dead husbands.

"Fancy a cup of tea with me, my dear old friend?" Belle reached for Annie's hand and patted it.

Annie was not sure what the sudden burst of affection meant, but it would be nice to take a break. "I'll bring our tea into the parlor," she said, squeezing Belle's hand.

"I'll put away my things." Belle removed her peach organza hat and stepped toward her room. A fit of coughing stopped her. She reached for the door frame and leaned against it.

"Belle?" Annie rushed to her side.

"It's the infernal dust. How on earth do you stand it?" She waved Annie off. "I'm fine, the tea will help. Good and hot now, mind you."

Annie bit her tongue. *Yes ma'am,* her mind screamed. Where did Belle get the idea she could boss her around? Even friendship couldn't wipe away the stigma of divorce and working for a living. Belle might look down on the very thing that made Annie proud. She'd survived, and she provided for her family. If things continued to improve, she'd be able to leave a secure future for them.

She calmed as she put the tea tray together with a few sugar cookies. What did it matter? Belle would return to Atlanta soon. There was nothing to keep her here.

Belle was waiting for her as she entered the parlor.

Annie poured Belle's tea, which was greeted with

a business-like nod, as she'd likely done a hundred times to her servants in Atlanta.

"You know, your Chef Fournier is a beacon for things to come. He's bringing a higher standard of things to this forsaken country." Belle poured a bit of tea into her saucer and blew across it.

Annie set her teacup down. "He's not *my* Chef Fournier, and what standard would that be?" She imagined tossing a cookie right at Belle's head.

"He brings a more refined attitude. He's just horrified at the gun toting men in this town. They will draw at the drop of a hat, for any small infraction. Chef Fournier is an educated man. Change is only wrought by such endeavors."

Annie picked up her teacup. She and the chef at least had disdain for guns in common. Her hand shook a bit, which made the cup rattle against the saucer. Change is what she prayed for. Maybe she should swallow her pride and listen. Annie's mother taught her to read, and that had made all the difference in her life. The school turned out some pretty good scholars, a few even headed to college in the east, but could Belle's comment about education mean something more? She sipped tea as she pondered a way to get Belle to expound on this theme. "We have a pretty good school here," Annie said.

"Of course, for children. And that's a start. But the adults of a community should continue their own education," she said, and then sniffed. "Well, women I mean. Most men don't concern themselves with such. Women are the true backbone of any community."

Belle nibbled at a sugar cookie.

"It's the men who hold office, run things. I can't even buy property without a man's signature." Annie was grateful to her lawyer friend Henson Jamison, but it still bothered her that she couldn't do it on her own.

"That will never change, I'm sure, but you know what they say; 'Behind every good man is a good woman.'" Belle shrugged her shoulders, as though everyone should know that.

That old idiom was something that Annie knew well. Things were not as strict regarding women in west Texas as it was in the north, or she wouldn't even be able to own the hotel. Still, she wanted Fort Stockton to be a place for those educated children to have something worth returning to, something with a future. She wanted a working woman to be respected. Her daughters deserved to be whatever they wanted. Her sons shouldn't have to fear for their lives just existing. There was a veil over the children of Barney Riggs. She wanted that lifted, and a clear path of their own choosing to open its way before them.

"I'm a member of Atlanta's Women of the Future. We gather to concern ourselves with the betterment of our city. We study current events, and plan ways to meet the needs of our citizens."

"Women of the Future," Annie repeated. This appealed to her.

CHAPTER 10

Annie wasn't sure how a tea party would advance Fort Stockton's prospects, but she gave herself to Belle's ideas and experience. They'd gather the women of the town and see what could be done.

The morning of the event arrived, and Belle awoke with enthusiasm Annie hadn't seen in her since she'd arrived.

"Leave it to me, darling. I'll take care of everything. You've already made the cookies and cake. Of course, we'll make the tea at the last." Belle bustled around the dining room with a pen and pad of paper.

Annie made the cookies, the cake, sandwiches, and set the table. What was left for Belle to do?

"I'm out of sugar, Belle, so I need to walk to the store. I'll return shortly."

"Fine, and then you can dress."

Annie's face flushed. She'd not thought to wear her best dress. This event was a serious matter to her, but she hadn't thought of finery for the occasion. "All right," she said, with a hope that her cheeks didn't show her embarrassment.

Annie returned from Kettler's store with the sugar to find her table setting completely replaced with Belle's china. So that's what was in one of the many trunks that kept arriving from Atlanta.

Belle came whirling out of the kitchen.

"Oh, darling, I didn't know where you keep you good dishes, so I just unpacked mine. You still had the table set for the cowboys, so I thought I'd lend you a hand."

"Um hum," Annie said, sliding past her into the kitchen. On her worktable sat a small cream pitcher and sugar bowl that matched Belle's china in the dining room table. Annie opened the sugar package and poured it in. Surely cream was cream everywhere, so she went to the pantry and retrieved her pitcher of cream and poured it into Belle's pitcher. She took it out to the dining room.

"Did you use the *Boston Cooking School Cookbook* for the cookies? They don't taste the same." Belle chewed with an expression like young Gene's when he tried to eat greens.

"Yes I did, but I didn't have any vanilla flavoring. I'm sure they'll do just fine. Everyone around here loves them," she said, regretting the emphasis on "loves." She mentally kicked herself for letting her irritation show. Belle was only trying to help her.

Annie also noticed that the crusts had been removed from the ham sandwiches. What a terrible waste. Belle better have put the crusts in the scrap bowl and not in the trash. She'd not quibble about it now. Too late.

"Who did you round up for this party?" Annie asked. Belle had made it her business to get to know the town's women.

"Well, besides your Maddie, I have Miss Kettler, the grocer's sister, I think they call her Patty. Then there's Sheriff Comhars wife, um," Belle stopped and squinted her eyes in thought.

"Caroline," Annie said.

"Yes, that's it, and Frank is bringing the station manager's wife, she's Philomena Jones, I think. Right?"

Annie nodded. "And my sister Mary. Also I invited Susanna Martin."

"That's eight, with you and I. Too bad your friend Henson's wife couldn't come to town for this. A lawyer's wife would be a plus." She counted off on her fingers.

"And Callie," Annie added.

"I thought little Callie would serve our tea," Belle said.

"No, she's to be a guest, and I already mentioned it to Doña Matilde."

Belle's surprise distorted her face, her eyebrows raised, and her mouth gaped open. She cocked her head for a few seconds, and then her face softened. "But there are only eight matching chairs." She dismissed the whole idea with a wave of her hand.

"I can add two straight backs from the parlor." Annie stepped toward the parlor and returned with the chairs.

Belle had her hands fisted on her hips. "But it won't match."

Annie squeezed the chairs in between two dining room chairs with a resolute thud. She would not allow Belle to bring her prejudices into her hotel. If Callie and

Matilde weren't welcome, the event would not take place. She crossed her arms and gave Belle a firm look.

"All right, dear, of course. Things are different here," Belle condescended, and then flitted around the table like a hummingbird, arranging and adjusting, her cheeks red as a cardinal.

Annie decided not to put on her best dress. It would make Callie feel more comfortable, and perhaps it would serve to irritate Belle, which Annie seemed moved to do. She walked out the back door. "Callie, I'd like you to come in and have tea with Mrs. Clark and I, and a few others." Annie encountered another surprised face. "Well, come on, then."

"I'm used to your kindness, Mrs. Annie, but I don't know about your friends."

Annie held out her hand.

Callie stood, took her hand, and followed her in.

Maddie and Mary were just sitting down at the table.

"This is nice, Mama. Is there anything we can do to help?" Maddie asked.

"I think it's all done, thanks to Belle." Or rather, no thanks to Belle. Annie sat down at the head of the table after seating Callie next to her on the left.

Doña Matilde slipped into the room in her usual quiet way, nodding hello to everyone.

Annie put her on her right. This left the rest of the chairs, including the two unmatched chairs for Belle's "distinguished" guests.

Belle seated herself at the other end of the table.

Caroline Comhars and Patty Kettler came in

together. They both flinched at the sight of Callie but didn't comment. They took the last two matching chairs. Philomena Jones came in, sat in the unmatched chair, and appeared nonplussed.

"We're ready for you to serve the tea, Annie," Belle said.

Annie opened her mouth to say that Susanna had not yet arrived, but Abel Martin came into the dining room. "I'm sorry, Mrs. Riggs, but Mama isn't feeling well and sends her re, re, um, regrets." He pulled at his shirt collar and swallowed. No doubt his shyness took a toll in the presence of so many women.

"Oh, all right, is there anything I can do?" Annie asked, taking a handful of cookies from the tray and wrapping them in a napkin. She stood, walked over to the boy, and handed him the cookies.

"She said she just needs to rest, and for me not to stay here a minute longer than it took to bring you the message. I'll be going. Thanks for the sweets." He walked out, and did not look back.

Annie smiled. At least he had a few cookies if he ever got a break.

Belle stood and removed the extra chair. "The tea, Annie."

"I'll give you that honor," Annie said. Irritation flushed through her chest. Just what was this, anyway?

Belle's eyes widened. She stared at Annie, but remained unmoved.

"I'll do it Mama," Maddie said.

Annie breathed a sigh of relief.

Maddie went into the kitchen.

An uncomfortable silence ruled the table, but Annie didn't care. Uppitiness was not what she had in mind for community improvement.

Maddie returned with the tea and served Callie first, which made perfect sense to Annie, since Callie was the closest to her as she came out of the kitchen.

Belle went white around her lips. She coughed into her lace handkerchief. "Guests, first, dear Maddie, of course." She twisted the handkerchief in her hands. "Country folks aren't familiar with city traditions," she said to the gathered wives of Fort Stockton.

The confused expressions made Annie think they wondered who Belle was calling "country folks."

Maddie stopped and looked at Annie, who shook her head slightly. No use starting something. She'd give Belle an earful later. Maddie continued pouring around the table, then set the teapot in front of Annie.

The women began serving themselves the sandwiches and cookies from the serving trays.

"Oh, Annie, these sandwiches are delicious," Philomena said. "Do you have a sick sow? I find that bread crusts seem to settle their stomach. It sure makes these sandwiches look pretty, though. You killed two birds with one stone."

Annie stifled a laugh. "Yes, bread crusts are a good remedy for pigs."

Belle nearly choked on a sip of tea, and her face blushed a shade of red that Annie had never seen before.

"It does work," Caroline said. "Just bread and water. But I wouldn't have used fresh bread. I would have used scraps. I keep feeding them scrap bread and water until they stop throwing up."

Belle coughed and set her teacup down.

Annie ventured a side glance at Doña Piña. The old woman sipped her tea but she had a decided twinkle in her eye and a faint upturn of lips. Annie contemplated whether she would continue to contribute to the pig conversation just to watch Belle's face change color. She didn't have to.

"What do you do with all the slop while you wait for the pigs to get well?" Philomena asked.

Caroline opened her mouth to answer.

Belle intervened. "I was hoping you ladies would consider an idea I have," Belle said.

"Oh? What did you have in mind?" Patty said, speaking for the first time.

"Our little town is on the verge of blossoming. We need some improvements to some of the landscape in town, make it more of a nice place to visit. Maybe form a ladies education group to discuss the current topics in the country and the state. We could call it the Fort Stockton Ladies Aid Society."

Our little town? Did this mean that Belle wasn't returning to Atlanta?

"I thought Ladies Aid was a group to sew clothes for missionaries, raise money for the poor, things like that," Philomena said.

"It is, and we could do all that. We could meet once a month for tea and decide what we want to do, and plan how we will implement it." Belle raised to her full sitting height; her hands folded in front of her.

"Essentially, we already do that, just not in an organized way," Patty said.

"Yes, we got together and sewed for Philomena's new baby. It was fun. We made the cutest little things," Caroline said.

Everyone, save Belle, smiled and nodded.

"But think of how much more we could do if we met regularly and got organized," Belle said.

The women looked at one another but didn't answer.

"Well, at least think about it," Belle said, and reached for her teacup. "This has gone cold, Maddie. Would you bring some more hot water?"

Maddie said, "Yes, ma'am," and left the table.

"Mrs. Clark, could I ask you a question about your time at the Fort?" Patty asked.

"Why, certainly dear," Belle said, her color returning to normal.

"Is that story true, the one about the feud between some of the officer's wives?"

"Well, I do know a story, a rumor actually, but it actually happened at Fort Davis," Belle said. "Russell brought the story back here after a visit to that Fort."

"Oh, tell us, please," Philomena interjected.

"Well, there was this officer's wife who hailed from Boston. She brought with her the finest clothes, which were completely inappropriate for this climate. She was constantly giving off airs and parading around the grounds with a tiny pistol hanging from a charm bracelet. Well, it really got on the nerves of an officer's wife from Arkansas. She was quite plain, in dress and in manners, but she had a terrific sense of humor. One day she donned her calico skirt, dolled up her hair in the latest fashion, and then paraded around the grounds with a full-sized service revolver hanging from her wrist." Belle sat back, a contented grin on her lips.

The ladies laughed and applauded.

Annie had heard that story and had to laugh alongside the others. She may be completely miffed with her friend, but she had to admit she could hold the attention of an audience. "Belle knows some officer's wives' stories that fall a little closer to home, if she remembers," Annie said, remembering the time Belle's bloomers were stolen off the clothesline behind their quarters.

Belle bored a hole in Annie with her stare. "Perhaps another time," she said, acid lacing her tone.

Again, an awkward silence fell among the ladies.

The food nearly gone, and with Maddie having gone around the table with tea for the third time, Annie began to wish they would leave. She had to get dinner cooked before the afternoon got away from her.

"Have any of you met the girl that the livery man married and brought here?" Belle asked. She set her saucer on top of the teacup.

The women looked at each other, but before Annie could stop her, Belle pressed on. "Her clothes look as if they came out of the missionary barrel, and I do mean the very bottom. She has a tooth missing, right in front, and it makes her talk with a lisp, or lithp, as she would say." Belle laughed at her little joke.

"Well, I..." Philomena began.

Annie tried to get Belle's attention, but she pressed on.

"I met her at Kettler's store, and I tell you, she smells like the horses that her husband boards." Belle laughed again, but the lack of response turned her cheeks red again.

"Yes, I've met her," Philomena said. "She's my sister, and I'd hoped for a more pleasant welcome than that." She rose and took her leave, none too gently.

Caroline stood. "Let me help you clear the dishes, Annie." She took up an armful of plates and rushed to the kitchen.

Maddie rose. "I'll help you, Mrs. Comhars."

"My brother is expecting me. Thanks for...the invitation," Patty said, and she left hurriedly as well.

"Gotta get home, Annie. I'll come by later and help you with dinner." Mary got up to leave.

Annie and Belle peered at one another from opposite ends of the table.

"I…I didn't know. I was decidedly charming to the livery's woman when I met her. I should let Mrs. Jones know," Belle said.

"I don't think that will help," Annie said.

"What would?" she asked.

"A sincere, heartfelt apology, might, and I emphasize *might* get you in her good graces again," Annie said.

"An apology? Well, indiscreet as it was, every word was true." Belle snuffed her nose, and stood.

Caroline came out of the kitchen. "I'll be seeing

you ladies. I enjoyed, um, the tea and food."

"But we didn't decide on the Fort Stockton Ladies Aid Society," Belle said.

"I think we'll just leave things the way they are for now. Good day." Caroline took her leave.

"I agree," Annie said.

"But what about your desire to change the reputation of your family? Promoting education, and the like?" Belle asked.

"This is not what I had in mind, and I don't remember you ever being so unkind," Annie said.

Belle stalked to her room in a huff, leaving Annie to finish clearing the table.

"I'll help you, Mrs. Annie." Callie smiled.

Annie had nearly forgotten that Callie was there. She'd not breathed a word since she came into the dining room an hour before.

"Not at all. You are my guest today. Thank you, just the same."

Callie ignored Annie and filled her arms with remaining the dishes and teacups, and then went into the kitchen to help Maddie finish up.

Doña Matilde rose from the table and stepped toward Annie. She kissed her on the cheek. "Did you pray about this first, mija? I don't think so." She tiptoed out of the hotel.

Annie could not recall ever seeing Doña Matilde Piña try and stifle a laugh.

As irritating and equally amusing as the whole thing turned out to be, Annie still felt frustrated about the state of her dreams. Something about Belle's version of refinement left a bad taste in her mouth.

"There'll be some education come, Mrs. Annie, when the train comes. Lem's been telling me the train gon' come through here. He said it will bring the whole wide world to Fort Stockton. That'll help them younguns."

The fact that Callie called him Lem delighted her.

Callie stayed in her cabin for a few days after Lem tried to explain the truth to her, but then she came out and went about her business, although she said very little.

Lem had taken on a job at Henson's ranch to give Callie time to make up her mind. Would he return to Atlanta and take Callie with him?

Maybe Callie would be all right. But as far as the train coming; she'd believe it when she saw it with her own two eyes. Always lots of talk, but no action.

Her little love Gene came barging into the room. No holding back for this child. Her youngest son reminded Annie of her younger self. Always rarin' to go.

"Mama, will you read dis book to me?" He threw his arms around her knees.

"Of course, my little man. Let me help Miss Callie with the dishes, and I'll be out in two shakes. Wait here, Gene, all right?" She picked him up, pecked him on the cheek, and set him in a chair at the table. "I'll be right back." She set some cookies on a plate for him.

"Yes, ma'am." He turned his attention to his little paperback book as he munched a cookie.

A few minutes later she returned to him, for

Maddie and Callie had everything well in hand. The biscuits could wait a few minutes while she read to the little boy who held her heart in the shine of his eyes. She found him engrossed in his book, in fact, his eyes were wide with fear.

"What have you got there, Gene?" She took the book from his hands.

The cover depicted an artist's version of none other than Barney Riggs and touted a story inside about the Miller-Frazer feud. Darned dime novels!

"Where'd you get this, Gene?"

"Mr. Simmons give it to me. Said it was 'bout Pa." His bottom lip quivered. "I shouldn't a taken it?"

She set him in her lap. "It's all right, but I would ask you not to take things from Mr. Simmons, or anyone else at the saloon. Just keep walking. If it's important, they'll talk to me," she said, kissing the top of his head. She put the pamphlet in her apron pocket.

His sweet face turned to hers. "Is dat Pa shootin' those men in the head? Looks bloody and scary. Wasn't Pa a nice man, Mama?"

She would promptly wring Charlie Simmons neck, right after coming up with an answer for Gene. She took a deep breath, and then held him close. "Your father shot those men, that's right. But they were very, very bad men. Those bad men were making things very hard for everyone." Dear God, let that be enough for now. One day Gene would be old enough to read for himself. Could she paint the true picture, without inspiring more violence?

"So Pa was a hero? Yay!" He bobbed up and down

in her lap.

"He...did what had to be done." That time.

"I don't wanna read the book no more, Mama. The pictures are scary. I better take it back to Mr. Simmons." He slid off her lap to a stand and held out his pudgy little hand for the dime novel.

"You run along home, now. I'll return the book to Mr. Simmons," she said.

"Ain't we going to church, Mama?"

The chaos of the day caused Annie to forget that she and Gene had made a habit of going to church to light a candle for the family members that were away.

"That's right. I'll run an errand, and then we'll go to church."

She knew better than to march over to the saloon when in such an angry state. She went into the kitchen and put her biscuit dough together, pounding the life out of it.

Callie stood in the corner watching her. "I can finish, Mrs. Annie. You gonna make the dough too hard like that."

"You're right. I do have an errand to run," she said. She ran her hands under the pump, dried them, and then left the hotel. She crossed the street toward the saloon. A couple of men stood outside with their horses as she approached the door.

"Ma'am, you don't want to go in there. That's no place for a lady," one old cowboy said.

"You're right, I don't want to go in there, and thank you." She pushed open the door of the saloon.

The curious men followed her in.

"Charlie Simmons, what's the meaning of you giving my son your outrageous dime novel. The pictures alone frightened him," she said.

Charlie stayed behind the bar. He continued drying whiskey glasses and didn't answer her.

She took a step toward him. "I mean it. What stunt are you trying to pull?"

He did not make eye contact. "He may as well know the truth about his pappy, that he was a hero around these parts. You should prepare yourself for the little apple of your eye to find out his mama had our hero shot to death, just so she could get her hands on his money."

She heard the door open and rushing boots.

Frank stood beside her.

"You all right, Mrs. Riggs?" he asked.

"I'm fine, thank you, Frank."

"If you ask me, it's Mrs. Riggs that's the murderer. Just what else got destroyed when you hired out your own son-in-law to do your killin' for you? How's your relationship with that daughter of yorn since everyone blames her husband for killing the man that put down the Miller gang?"

Follow your own advice, Annie. Walk away. If only Barney had been able to walk away when he got angry. He'd still be here with me. She never took her gaze off Charlie.

He laughed. "Yeah, cat got your tongue cuz you know I'm right," he said.

Annie took another step forward, and then stopped. She put her hand in her apron pocket.

A collective gasp, chairs scraping across the floor,

and then dead silence.

Charlie reached his hand under the bar but left it there.

"Now, there ain't no call for anything further, Mrs. Riggs. I'll take care of this," Frank said.

"How you gonna do that? You ain't got no gun," someone called out from behind.

Frank took Annie by the arm, led her outside the saloon, and across the street. "You go on back home, Ma'am. I'll be back in time for supper."

She let the cool of the evening, and the chores ahead calm her down. She prayed Charlie wouldn't shoot an unarmed man. She watched outside the hotel entrance, but didn't see any activity to speak of, except her hotel guests leaving the saloon and coming across the street, expecting their supper.

Callie had spread the sideboard with a pile of biscuits, a kettle of pinto beans, and a tray of sliced ham. She'd also set out a tray of bread slices and a pitcher of syrup.

Gene sat at the table eating a biscuit.

As the men came in and started filling their plates, one of them sidled up to Annie.

"Looks like young Frank Hankins took care of things. Don't know how he did it without a gun."

"How *did* he do it?" Annie asked.

"Looks like a gentleman's agreement. They got off in a corner and was talking passionate like. Frank must've threatened him, and with Frank bein' younger and all, maybe Charlie believed it. Wouldn't be hard for Frank to get his hands on a gun around here."

"I believe you, all but the gentleman part." Annie breathed a sigh of relief. What could she do? If Charlie would just settle down and stop spitting angry words, she might could fix it. But she wasn't about to tell him anything about the land Barney wanted to give him until he stopped antagonizing her. It was in Charlie's hands, that's what. She'd have to speak to Henson and see if there wasn't something he could do about Charlie's accusations, make him stop calling her a murderer. Maybe she'd have Henson draw up a paper giving Charlie the land Barney promised him. Maybe that would shut him up.

The next morning Annie thought over all things over coffee on the veranda. Matilda Piña's ascension up the steps pulled Annie from her thoughts.

"To what do I owe this lovely visit?"

Doña Matilda's eyes shone and her smile brightened Annie's mood. "Ah, mija, the new priest is arriving today. We've received a telegram. The Hijas are preparing his rooms in the little corner house behind the church, and I thought you and I could prepare a meal for him!"

Annie coughed as a dry throat crept up and nearly choked her. He was really coming? Oh, how her prayers had contained mixed emotions. Would he reject her the way the "righteous" women of Fort Stockton had? No amount of devoted service had changed her position in their eyes.

"Are you all right? You've gone white, whiter than usual." Doña Matilde sat in the rocker next to her.

Whiter than usual? What? Her coughing fit turned

to laughter. "I don't think I've ever heard you make a joke." She shook off her trepidation. Besides, she'd given up trying to please anyone long ago. Her Heavenly Father was in her heart, and she served him out of love and gratitude.

"What joke. *Tu eres positivamente pailda!* Um, very pale, mija. You are working too hard." She placed her hand on Annie's forehead.

"I'm quite well, you just surprised me with the news. I didn't think it would ever happen. Of course, I will help you with a meal. What were you thinking?"

"I have started some frijoles, and I will make fresh tortillas and some salsa. Perhaps some ham, and a peach cobbler from you?"

"I can do that. The Padre is Mexican?" Annie mentally discerned whether she had the supplies for what she just promised.

"No, I think French, by the name. It is Decorme. But what does it matter?" Matilde's puzzled expression tickled Annie.

"It does not matter at all, but what might matter is the heat of the salsa. You do tend to like it hot, very hot." Annie leaned over the rocking chair arm put her arm around her friend.

"Ah, *si, muy picoso*. I'll go light, pero I will warn him anyway."

"We don't want him to regret his appointment from the beginning. There is plenty of concern for his ministry here without tearing up his stomach."

"Very true. But it will be glorious to have a regular priest, regular sermons, blessings, sacraments. Our prayers have been answered, my Annie. Well, if I'm to make tortillas, I must get home. I'll come by for you around 5:00 PM this evening, and we'll go together." Matilde stood and headed for the door, her heels clicking with a swift gait toward her tasks.

"Well, goodbye then." Annie smiled. Matilde's excitement warmed Annie's heart. The dear old woman had carried the spiritual responsibility of the entire town. Perhaps the priest could interest the men of Fort Stockton in the church.

The afternoon wore on with delightful preparations for the new Father Decorme. Annie had forgotten to ask if he was old or young, and from what order. She put her cobbler in the oven and then sat down with a cup of coffee. Her thoughts turned to the traveling priests they'd had from time to time. Her throat constricted again as she remembered the dismissive looks she'd received. Undoubtedly the padres had been schooled in her past by the faithful women of Fort Stockton. Meetings took place that Annie only heard about after.

As the clock in the foyer struck 5:00 PM, Matilde came in with a large basket over her arm. "Ready? He has arrived. The Hijas will sing a hymn for him. I'm sure he is hungry after his long trip from El Paso."

"I have my offerings here in this basket, but I'm afraid I can't go. I have too much to do here. I'll meet him at Mass." She couldn't make eye contact with the woman who knew her so well.

Frank walked into the kitchen just in time. "Frank can carry my basket. Would you mind accompanying

Doña Piña to the church, Frank?"

"I ain't never stepped inside a church, Mrs. Riggs."

That sentence was met with a momentary silence from both of the women.

"I see. Well, there's a first time for everything. It's not a service anyway, you'll just be delivering some food to the new priest." She picked up the basket and handed it to Frank. His expression reminded her of the time her brother came face to face with a rabid dog.

Matilde took a step toward Annie. "Have you imagined something unhappy in that normally smart head of yours? Something to be afraid of?"

"Of course not." Annie avoided her gaze. "I've just got to get dinner ready for my guests. You can come and tell me all about it later. Better get on with you both now."

Doña Piña's lips straightened into a grim line. Her brown eyes darkened even more.

Annie waited for the lecture that didn't come.

Doña marched toward the door.

Frank followed, but not nearly with as much energy.

Annie pushed down guilt and busied herself with dinner preparations. She washed the dishes, knowing that Callie would wonder why in the world she would take that job away from her. She kept occupied with sundry tasks until the sun went down, and then took to her rocking chair on the veranda.

The cool breeze helped bring clarity to her thinking. She had certainly done what Matilde had implied, imagined something to be afraid of. Would her life change much if the priest did not accept her? Of course not, although there would be much more to be left out of. Well, he couldn't exclude her from helping with the service of the Hijas, could he? Would he? Would Matilde's word hold any weight? She'd just have to go to her friend in the morning and apologize, admit to her the truth that she already knew.

Her thoughts turned toward going inside and finishing up the chores in the kitchen.

A very young man in a black priest's garb rounded the corner from the church and approached the bottom step, her cobbler dish under his arm. "Mrs. Riggs?" he asked with a tip of his rimmed hat.

"Why, yes, and you must be Father Decorme," Annie answered. Her palms grew moist and she resisted the urge to run them down her skirt.

"May I come up for a brief visit? I want to thank you for the ham and cobbler." He held the glass dish up with both hands.

"Of course." Why did she feel so uncomfortable? He couldn't have been more than twenty-five years old.

He bounded up the steps with the vim that only the youth can deliver. He sat in the rocker beside her. "I suppose you notice the cobbler dish is empty. I'm afraid I ate the whole thing. Delicious! I will have to repent for my gluttony," he said, rubbing his stomach over his cassock.

She smiled. "I'm so glad you enjoyed it. How are you finding your rooms? The Hijas worked hard to make it nice for you."

"Very nice, very nice. I admit I'm pretty exhausted, but I couldn't let the sun go down without meeting you and thanking you for the wonderful meal." He leaned back in the rocker, and seemed to let rest wash over him.

"We're so glad that you're here. Doña Piña is almost solely responsible for the spiritual training in this area. I think she is more grateful than anyone for your presence." Annie glanced at his youthful face. His short dark hair lay straight below his hat, and his green eyes and high cheek bones fashioned a very pleasant face, if not handsome. She could see plain as plain that she would have to help Matilde to fatten him up. Thin as a rail!

"I understand that the men need some nudging in the area of the church. I thought I'd start with getting up a game of football." He closed his eyes, spread out his legs and began to rock.

Football? Well, the men might enjoy that and be more open to being involved in the church. At least that's what she thought the padre might be thinking. If he'd fallen asleep, she'd not ask him now.

"You're awfully quiet, Mrs. Riggs," he said, without opening his eyes.

"I thought you might be asleep," she whispered.

"Oh, certainly not, that would be rude. I am sorry, but my weariness is great. I just thought to rest a moment."

"No problem at all. Would you like a cup of tea? I find when I'm overtired that a cup of chamomile settles me right down." She stood and motioned to the front door.

"That would be lovely. I'm dying to see the inside of the hotel, anyway. I've heard many wonderful things about it from the pastors who visit here and then come to El Paso."

Gladness sprouted in her heart. She worked so hard, and rarely heard a compliment. People did praise her biscuits and peach cobbler, but there was so much more to running hotel. She found Father Decorme rather easy to talk to. Perhaps her silly fears were unfounded.

She left him in the parlor while she went to prepare the tea. He hummed something that sounded like a hymn. It would be nice for someone to bring the newer melodies to Fort Stockton. Faithful Matilde knew many, but they were ancient. The tune the padre hummed had a haunting melody. "Is that a new hymn?" Annie asked as she brought in the tea tray.

"Oh, certainly not. It's from the eighth century I believe. 'O Come O Come Emmanuel." He proceeded to sing the words.

What a lovely voice! "I know those words, but with a different melody." She went to her piano bench and shuffled through the sheet music until she found the one she wanted.

Father Decorme stood beside her and sang along.

"Yes, I've heard that melody too. Perfect hymn for Christmas, don't you think?"

"I agree," she said. "Let's have our tea so that you can get to bed, young man." Her tendency to mother everyone, to Barney's chagrin, crept into her heart.

Truly, her prayers had been answered.

"Mrs. Riggs, I've heard so much about you. I'd really like to talk to you about your past. And also, there's something about Frank Hankins. But I'm very tired. I'll come and see you on another day." He stood and stifled a yawn.

"You want to discuss my past?" Her joy deflated. "Is that really necessary?" She didn't need to be told of her inferior qualifications for church work. And what had Frank done?

"I'll see you soon, and thank you so much for the cobbler, ham, and the lovely visit. Thank you for the tea. I'll see myself out. Goodnight, Mrs. Riggs." He took his leave.

Annie sat motionless in her chair. Nothing ever changed.

Chapter 11

Annie did not look forward to a talk about her past with Father Decorme, but she'd promised Gene a trip to the church. She took Gene's hand and they started down the road. "Got any peppermints in your pocket, Mama?"

"You'll just have to wait and see, young man."

"When we gets to the church, let's light a candle for Mr. Frank," Gene said.

"Let's do, but why, Gene?"

Gene loved Frank Hankins. Frank sometimes played with him as if they were both kids.

"Cuz I went to his room last night to see if he wanted to play, and he looked plum scared, like somebody died or something. Did somebody die?" Gene looked up at Annie.

"He may have been thinking about his family. He must miss them. Yes, let's light a candle and pray for Frank."

They stepped inside the church and approached the candles. Annie lit candles for Beau, who would soon be coming to take Maddie to New Mexico, for Jack on the cattle drive, and for Liza Mae, Thad, and Sarah, Callie, Lem and his family, and then she crossed herself.

Gene imitated her and then they knelt at the altar. Annie couldn't help but smile at Gene's chubby little hands, folded together in prayer with his eyes closed.

She wondered what he requested for Frank. She said her prayers, and wondered if Father Decorme would appear. She'd certainly not go looking for him. When they finished, she led Gene back to the hotel.

Maddy arrived to take him home to Doña Piña's so that they could work.

Henson Jamison rushed into the hotel with his young son in his arms, both of them covered in blood.

"Annie, he's cut himself on a lathe, it's pretty bad. I need your help."

"Of course, bring him to the kitchen table." She rushed ahead of him and yanked the tablecloth away.

Henson set the boy down.

A black neck-tie was tied around his upper left arm. A bloody cloth was wrapped around his arm just above the elbow and soaked in blood. His eyes were closed and he didn't move.

"Liam was playing on the plow when I pulled up to the ranch. He jumped off, but landed on the blade. I'm afraid he'll lose his arm, if not his life. I wrapped him with my night shirt, unhitched one of the horses from the buggy, and headed right here. Hepatica is beside herself. We have no medicines or anything at the ranch."

"Get Callie for me, and then tend to your horse. I'll see what I can do." She forced her voice to remain calm, but the boy was already pale from blood loss.

Frank appeared in the kitchen. "I'll get Callie, and

then I'll tend to Mr. Jameson's horse," he said.

Annie nodded, crossed herself, said a quick prayer, and then unwrapped the wound. Her stomach lurched at the sight of the deep wound. She could see bone.

Henson stood over his boy's head, fear emanating from his expression.

"Henson, there's a satchel of medical supplies under my bed. Please retrieve it for me."

He hurried out without a word and returned in minutes with the worn, black leather satchel.

Annie began to clean the wound with fresh cloths as Frank and Callie came in the side door.

"Callie, put the large kettle on. Frank, help me get his shirt off. Henson, go to your office and try to calm yourself down."

"Yes, ma'am," Callie said.

"Yes, ma'am." Frank's tone was a little shaky.

"I'm not leaving my boy."

"Looks bad, Mrs. Riggs. Can you save the arm?" Frank asked with a steadier voice as he lifted the boy's tunic shirt and reached to pull out the good arm.

Annie cut the sleeve off of the wounded arm, and they both gently lifted the shirt over his head. Annie pressed hard on the wound with both hands. "Frank, open the satchel and find a small case. Get a needle and a roll of thread you'll find there, and see if you can thread the needle."

He wasted no time in attempting that task, but it was no use.

"I can do it, Mrs. Annie," Callie said, as the kettle

began to spew steam.

Henson remained at his son's head, stroking his hair. A tear dropped on Liam's forehead.

"Frank, put these cloths in the sink, pour the boiling water over them, and then as soon as you can handle them, bring them to me."

He stepped to the stove and a moment later brought the rags to Annie.

She wiped the wound with the hot rags, but blood continued to drip and pool on the kitchen floor. She held the wound together as best she could, and took the threaded needle from Callie. As carefully as she could, she began to sew the flesh together.

The boy's eyes fluttered, and he cried out.

Henson lowered his lips to Liam's ears. "It's all right, son, you'll be fine. Try to be still. Pa is here."

"Frank, hold him down." Annie kept her tone calm.

Frank laid his arm across Liam's chest. "It's all right, boy, Mrs. Annie will get you fixed up."

Liam opened his eyes, blinked erratically, and then began to cry.

"Don't move now, Mrs. Annie needs you to be still," Henson said.

Callie held down his legs, because he'd begun to thrash and kick.

Annie sewed the wound together as tightly as she could. The boy passed out, which made it easier for her to work, but the blood made it so slippery. Callie took hot cloths and dabbed at the blood as Annie worked on the wound. Finally, it was held together, and the blood oozed less.

Annie pressed on the wound a bit longer, took a deep breath, and then untied the tie. If Henson hadn't thought to do that, they'd already be standing over a dead child. Blood flowed for a few seconds but then stopped. She did what she could to clean him up, and then wrapped the wound in fresh, clean cloths from the satchel. A small stain of blood appeared, but she continued to wind the cloth around his arm, and then tucked it under the bundle. "Callie, I think I have one of Gene's night shirts in the bottom drawer of my dresser. Would you get it please?"

Callie nodded and returned with the long-sleeved, white, night shirt.

Annie cut off the left sleeve with her kitchen shears, and she, Henson, and Frank worked to get the shirt on the boy, who was still unconscious.

Callie pulled off his shoes, socks, and trousers.

"Frank, can you lift him?"

"Yes, please take him to my room, and put him in the bed." Hensen jerked his head towards the room he kept at the hotel.

Annie picked up the satchel and she and Callie followed as Frank carried Liam through the back door and out onto the porch. His boots scraped across the threshold.

Callie opened the door to Henson's room, and Frank stepped inside. Annie pulled the quilts back and Frank laid the boy on the bed. Annie put a pillow underneath his arm to keep it elevated.

"I'll clean up that kitchen table, Mrs. Annie,"

Callie said.

"Thank you."

Annie covered Liam with the quilt, and then stroked his forehead. He felt hot to her.

Henson sat on the bed and held his hand to Liam's cheek. "Will he be all right?"

"There's a good chance. He's got fever, though. I'll wash my hands and get some water and rags to try to bring it down. He will be fine here, Henson. You should go home and reassure Hepatica."

"She would've come with me, but young Bart is down with the measles. I'm not leaving him, though."

Annie left Henson to be with his son while she went for cool water and rags.

Frank sat at the kitchen table.

"Thanks for your help, Frank. Did Callie go home?"

"Yes, ma'am. Callie said to tell you, to fetch her if she was needed."

Annie perused her kitchen. Callie had left it spotless. Bless her.

"It'll be a long night for Hepatica Jameson," Annie said as she sat across the table from Frank.

"Would you like me to ride out to the Jameson ranch and reassure her?" Frank asked.

Annie thought for a moment. "You could get there before sundown if you leave now. Perhaps Doña Matilde could go with you, she knows the way. Maybe Hepatica will allow her to stay with her Bart so she can come to town. Lem is there, but I'm sure a woman's presence would help. Some such arrangement, anyway."

"All right," Frank said.

Annie stood. "I'll walk over to Matilde's and ask her while you get the buggy and horses ready."

"Yes ma'am," he said, and left the room.

Annie didn't take time to grab her shawl but walked outside and across the block to Doña Matilde's house. Her good friend answered immediately, and after hearing the dilemma, agreed right away to go with Frank. Within half an hour Annie waved them off as they headed down the road toward the ranch.

She checked on Liam and found both he and his father asleep on the bed. Annie stood in the doorway and prayed. She wrapped her shawl tight and took up watch in Henson's rocker. During the night she checked his arm and forehead for signs of increasing fever. Just as the sun came up she decided to bath him with cool water.

"Henson, we've got to get his fever down," she said, shaking his leg.

Liam had slept fitfully throughout the night.

"Of course," Hensen said, and sat up. He felt Liam's arm and forehead.

Annie went for fresh cloths and water and returned to find Henson unbuttoning the night shirt. The two of them bathed him front and back repeatedly with Annie going back and forth for fresh water.

Liam cried in pain. Annie brought him a piece of dry toast but he could barely chew it for crying. She decided to give him some of Mrs. Winslow's soothing syrup to make him sleep.

After his dressing was changed and he sipped some water containing the syrup, he calmed, and then finally went back to sleep.

"Frank and Doña Matilde went to the ranch last night. Matilde offered to stay with Bart so Frank should be returning with Hepatica this morning."

"I'm relieved to hear that, thank you. I'm glad she'll find her son living when she arrives. Thank heaven."

"Yes, thank the Father for getting us through the night. I think I will go to St. Joseph's and do just that. Maddie will be along directly to get breakfast going. She'll see that you have something to eat."

Annie walked to the church with a thankful heart, although weary to the bone. She lit a candle and knelt at the altar. After her prayers, her thoughts went to Frank. Such a helpful young man. There was so much good in him. But she couldn't shake the feeling that something wasn't right. She stood and nearly walked right into Father Decorme. "Oh! I didn't know you were standing there."

"I just walked up. I've been to the hotel and prayed for the boy. Your Miss Callie came by early this morning to inform me."

"Ah, good. I think he will recover if we can get his fever down," Annie said. She tried to step aside to take her leave.

Father Decorme stepped in front of her.

Here it comes.

"Mrs. Riggs, some of the Fort Stockton citizens have told me about your former husbands and their escapades," he said, crossing his arms.

"Yes, well, it happened. I, well, I did the best I could with them. They were abusive. Divorce was the only option to save my life, and the future of my children. I regret the divorces, and I know it was sin, but, well, there was no other option."

"I cannot imagine the horrors you endured, but in Christ you are forgiven." He put his hand on her shoulder and looked into her eyes. "I hope you will put it behind you. When you come to confession I hope I hear about current infractions, not those of long ago." He smiled.

Tears welled up in Annie's eyes. How did he know? Did Matilde tell him of her constant fear of rejection by God? She always felt His presence and depended on Him with all her heart. She had worked so hard for the church hoping beyond hope that it would be enough. She didn't really care that she was still not always invited to the events the ladies put on. It didn't matter so much what they thought. But what did God think? Everyone thought her so strong, but if they only knew how insecure she felt sometimes. "Thank you, Father. My head knows it. It has not yet reached my heart."

Father Decorme seemed to emanate understanding. With both hands on her shoulders he prayed for her. They both crossed themselves. "We will work on your heart, then," he said.

Her heart was so full she couldn't respond. She just nodded and headed for the door. She turned, and with a grin, asked, "Current infractions?"

He laughed. “Everyone has them, including me. Oh, by the way, your young handyman, Frank.”

“Yes?” Annie stepped back inside the church.

“He never once made eye contact with me the entire time he was here with Doña Piña. I’m concerned about him, although I don’t know why yet.”

“Well, he told us he’d never been in church before. Perhaps the sight of a priest made him nervous.”

“Hm, maybe, but I sensed a deception of some kind. A fear of being found out. Guilt. Yes, that’s what I saw. I would just caution you to be careful.” He came alongside her, and they walked into the street.

Annie didn’t know what to say. Had she been ignoring her own questions about Frank?

The priest turned to head the opposite direction.

Annie walked back to the hotel. She checked on Liam and found him sitting up and sipping a cup of tea.

“The fever has broken. I don’t know how to thank you, Annie.” Henson stood and held both her hands in his.

“Spoken as though I don’t owe you for this very hotel.”

Liam smiled and in a weak little voice whispered, "Thank you.”

“Your mother will be here this evening, Liam. You can all stay here,” Annie said.

Liam’s little smile broadened.

Annie nodded and headed out of the room to do her chores.

CHAPTER 12

Abel Marten came crashing into the hotel.

Annie stepped from behind the desk.

"Mrs. Riggs, you've got to come."

"Your mama's time come, Abel?" Annie closed the guest book.

"Yes, ma'am, and she's hollerin to beat the band. Can you come?"

"I'll be right there. Go out back and hitch up my buckboard. I'll have things to carry." Annie rushed to her room to get her bag.

Abel pulled into the front of the hotel with the buckboard. He helped Annie into the wagon.

Frank was sitting on the veranda. He'd just returned from Henson's ranch with Hepatica.

Matilde had indeed stayed with Bart so his mother could come.

"Frank, I need you to go to my sister's house. Tell her to please come and look after the hotel with Maddie while I help Mrs. Marten with her baby." Annie squirmed into position on the seat and straightened her skirts.

"Yes, ma'am, Mrs. Riggs." He hopped down the steps, then turned toward Mary's house.

~*~

Annie and Abel arrived at the Marten's home in due time.

Suzanna had grown pale and quiet. She'd stopped pushing and was as limp as a dishrag.

"Suzanna, wake up, the pains have stopped. You need to rally. I'll do all I can to help, but you can't give up." Annie considered sending for someone else. She didn't want to see Suzanna die, and her child as well.

"Is she gonna be fine, Mrs. Riggs?" Abel's eyes were wide as saucers.

His fear strengthened Annie for the task. "You stay in the parlour."

She went into the bedroom, assessed the situation and then slapped Suzanna's face. "Suzanna, wake up, you've got to finish this job. You're almost there, I can see the baby's head. You've got to find the strength to push a few more times."

Suzanna's eyelids fluttered. She shook her head as though she didn't remember where she was. A pain came, and with a scream, she was all there again.

"Come on, Suzanna, push!" Annie pressed down as hard as she could to give the baby more room.

Suzanna screamed again and pushed.

The baby slid down far enough so that Annie could reach in and pull him out.

"It's a boy! You've got a boy," Annie said, as she cleared his throat, turned him upside down, and spanked him. His vigorous cry thrilled her.

Suzanna smiled but closed her eyes and slumped back, panting a bit before her breath evened out.

Annie felt her pulse. "That's right, Suzanna, you rest a bit. I'll get this little fella cleaned up and all pretty for you."

The door opened and Abel stuck his nose through.

"It's a baby brother for you, Abel, and your ma will be fine. She just needs to rest a bit."

"He sure does holler, don't he?"

Annie covered Suzanna. "Come on in and look at him. He's fine looking, and strong."

Abel came near and she laid the babe in his arms. "You take him and sit in the other room while I tend to your ma. Hold his head and neck now, just right."

"Yes, ma'am," Able said.

"Well, go on, he won't break," Annie said.

Suzanna lifted her head from the pillow. "He's all right? I heard you say it was a boy."

"He's just fine, Suzanna. Now I'll get you cleaned up and get you some broth. You'll need your rest for a bit, but then you'll be just fine. Abel is holding the child until we get this set to rights."

"Matthew," Suzanna said. "That was his father's name."

CHAPTER 13

Annie became more and more concerned about Belle. The slight and infrequent cough she had when she'd arrived in Fort Stockton had increased to a daily event. When Annie finished her chores the evening after Matthew Marten was born, she realized that Belle had never come out of her room. She tiptoed in to check on her, and she slept, or pretended to. Annie decided to gather her laundry. As she left the room with an armload of Belle's things, she tripped over the threshold and the laundry scattered before her.

She hurried to gather the mess lest she wake Belle, but was taken aback by a bloody handkerchief on the pile of laundry. Oh, no. No. It all made sense now. Her coughing, and her skin was so pale it was almost transparent. Annie must get her to the doctor in Pecos right away.

She let Belle sleep a few more hours, and then carried in a tray of tea and toast. She touched Belle's cheek.

Belle opened her eyes.

Annie helped her sit up. "You knew you were sick when you came here, didn't you Belle? Why haven't you gone to the doctor?" She primped and tucked the covers around her friend. "Here, have a sip of water."

"I thought the climate would help, and it did at first. When it began to worsen, I ignored it." She took another sip of water but then shook into a fit of coughing.

Annie handed her a clean handkerchief and noticed the drops of blood after Belle's coughing calmed. "Well, you should have come earlier. Winter is setting in."

"My physician in Atlanta claimed trying a dryer climate was my last chance. It is dry, but the dust, Annie, the dust." She coughed again. After a bit, she said, "I'm just having a bad day."

"Nevertheless, I'm sending for the doctor in Pecos. I'll have Maddie telegraph a message that he needs to come quickly." She held Belle's hand in hers.

"Just like me, right? Come to a place where there's no doctor close by when I'm dying of consumption." She started laughing, but nearly choked on her cough. "How," then she held her breath to try not to cough, but it came anyway. "How do you live in this god-forsaken place?"

Annie's beloved west Texas simply did not fit the word god-forsaken. "We do all right," Annie answered. She sat down on the bed. Belle settled, so Annie helped her lay down again, but propped her head up on a pillow. Annie lovingly soothed the covers in around her.

Belle turned her head toward the window. "I wish my children were here."

By the amount of blood Annie feared it was too late for that, poor dear. "I'll send them a telegram.

You'll have to rally so that you can entertain." They'd have to come for her anyway.

"Oh, there's no hurry. Maybe we can invite them for Christmas?" She snuggled down into the covers.

"I'll extend an invitation right away," Annie said.

Suddenly Belle grasped Annie by the blouse and pulled her face close to hers. Where had that energy come from?

"I don't want to die, Annie. I'm terrified."

Annie put her arms around her. "Sh, sh, dear Belle. You need to make your peace with God. You'll feel better." Annie opened the bottom drawer of Belle's nightstand and pulled out a rosary. She placed it in Belle's hand.

"I don't know what to do with this, Annie. I'm a Methodist. Well, Mama was."

"But you can pray, and you should."

"I always let the minister handle that," Belle said, but gasped. She could not catch her breath. "I've been used to having people serve me, someone to do the hard things. Now I find I have no one to take my place. I will have to come face to face with my Maker."

Annie remembered her attempts to share her faith with Belle in the old days. She'd just laughed it off. "Oh, but dear Belle, someone has already taken your place. Your Maker, as you say, provided Jesus Christ to take your place. You are not alone, even in death." Belle wasn't Catholic, but perhaps Father Decorme could help her, or Doña Matilda.

"Not now, I'm so tired. You pray with me Annie. You're the closest person I know to God. He'll listen to you." Belle grasped Annie's hands; the Rosary entwined between the two.

"Don't you understand, Belle? He listens to you, too."

"Please, Annie." Belle was beginning to look blue around the lips.

Annie sighed. "All right, dear. But only you can ask Jesus to come into your heart, Belle. You don't have to speak. You can pray silently for Jesus to save your soul." She whispered prayers over Belle, hoping she'd accept the gift that Christ had provided for her.

"Thank you, Annie. Do you remember the time we made cookies for the officers, and we forgot the sugar?" She laughed, but it caused her to cough.

"Of course, I do. Remember the looks on their faces, but they were too honorable to complain. It wasn't until I took a bite that I understood. They laughed at the look on my face, and then we were all laughing." She dipped a cloth in a bowl of water and dabbed the blood from Belle's lips. She moistened the cloth again and let it rest on Belle's forehead.

"I'd like to go to sleep now, Annie," Belle said in her "that will be all" tone of voice.

Annie grinned. Belle never changed. She hoped her heart had changed during prayer. She put the bowl and cloths on the tray with the toast and tea things, then stood and walked through the door. She turned to pull the door closed. "I'll send that telegram, Belle, you rest."

"They won't come," Belle said.

Annie frowned. Why wouldn't they? Her

condition was addling her thinking. "Of course they will."

She put away the tray things, and then walked to the telegraph office.

Your mother is very ill. Suggest you come right away. Stop.

A moment at St. Joseph's would be just the thing. She'd ask Father Decorme to talk to Belle. Annie lit a candle and dropped to her knees at the altar. She'd just have to have faith that Belle would make her peace with God. She wondered what it would be like to live a life of luxury, where everything centered around oneself. She thought about what a sweet, loving friend Belle had been as a girl. What had changed her? She opened her prayer book and pulled out a clipping she'd saved from the newspaper.

Wishes

If any line that I ever penned,
Or any word I have spoken,
Has comforted heart, of foe or friend--
In any way, why my life, I'll say
Has reaped the reward of labor.
If aught I have said, or written, has made
Gladder the heart o' my neighbor.
If any deed that I ever did
Lightened a sad heart's sorrow,
If I have lifted a drooping lid
Up to the bright to-morrow,
Though the world knows not, nor gives me a thought,

Nor ever can know, nor praise me,
Yet still I shall say, to my heart away,
That my life, and labor repay me.
If in any way I have helped a soul,
Or given a spirit pleasure,
Then my cup of joy, I shall think is full
With an overflowing measure.
Though never an eye, but the one on high
Looks on my kindly action,
Yet, oh my heart, we shall think of our part
In the drama, with satisfaction.

The poem by Ella Wheeler Wilcox suddenly magnified on the page. She'd been trying so hard to change Fort Stockton, to make a different world for her children. But with Belle's life slipping through like water in a sieve, a clearer mission presented herself. She couldn't change anything but herself. It wasn't her job to change Fort Stockton, it was only her job to love and serve as best she could. Oh, to come to the last hour of her life and feel used up in the service of others. Christ had already done everything, she need only to show His love to others. She rose from her knees with a new resolve.

Maddie met her at the door upon returning. "I'm sorry, Mama. I just checked on Belle. I'm afraid she's passed."

Annie's heart cried with sadness, but her eyes only burned.

Maddie embraced her.

"I'll go to her."

"You knew?" Maddie asked.

"I only just realized. She hid it well until recently."

Annie had her buried in the family area of the cemetery. It couldn't wait until she heard from Belle's family. But Belle had been right, they never came, nor returned the message. She didn't want to think about what had caused the rift in the relationships with Belle's sons. She would hold on to that moment when they held the Rosary together and prayed. Belle's death had changed Annie.

The event was the foundation of her new lease on life.

CHAPTER 14

A few days later as Annie and Gene left Mass, they found Frank walking toward them.

Gene ran toward Frank, who picked him up and swung him high in the air. Gene laughed and kicked his legs.

"You run on to the hotel, Gene, I'll be right there," Annie said.

Frank put him down and Gene ran off, giggling.

"Mrs. Riggs, I'd like to ask you a question," Frank said, holding his hat in one hand, but then passing it back and forth between both his hands. He seemed to find something on the ground very interesting.

"Oh, certainly," she said. "What's going on?"

"Oh, well, I wondered if you'd let me take you to the dance that's being planned at the park?"

She'd never seen him so nervous. "I'll be happy to dance with you, Frank, thank you."

He opened his mouth to speak but couldn't seem to find words. He rubbed a rough spot in the road with his boot. "Well, sure, but what I meant was, we could go together, you know, as, well, together."

What was this boy getting at? "If you are saying what I think you're saying, surely I'm wrong, but Frank Hankins, I hope I haven't given you any reason to think that we are more than, well, friends." She took a slight step back.

"You've been nothing but wonderful to me. You're not that much older than me. I'm a good hard worker, and I, I find I care about you. I could be the husband that helps you, that goes the distance." He managed to look her in the eye.

She hated to hurt him, but she wanted to be clear so he'd stop entertaining this idea. Maybe she'd let him get too close. But had he not seen that she could take care of herself? "Frank, I'm flattered. But I have had two husbands already, and I'm not looking for another. It always starts out sweet, but it never ends that way. I'm not interested in another relationship like that. We're friends, Frank. So far, my family who knows you feels the same friendship. Please, let's not talk of this any longer." Could these thoughts be what made him seem deceptive to Father Decorme?

"Drink ruined those men. I don't drink, and I don't carry a gun. You still have a long life ahead of you, and I don't want you to be alone. Won't you give me a chance?" He ventured to reach for her hand.

She took a breath to speak, but he lifted his hand to cup her cheek. He lifted her face toward him and tilted his face closer to hers. "Please don't say no, Mrs. Riggs, um, Annie."

Lost in his eyes for a second, she didn't stop him. Reason returned and she pulled away. "I can't promise you that, Frank." Why didn't she just say no?

"Please don't lock into an answer just yet. Promise me that." His eyes implored her.

"I can promise you," she began, and then stepped away, "one dance."

His grin looked like sunshine after a rain. "I'll take it. I'll see you there."

She watched him saunter down the street, and then she went inside the hotel. She sat down at the piano and tickled the keys gently, playing a random melody. Her mind replayed what just happened with Frank. Could she ever marry again? Frank was a hard worker, and respectful. She had empathy for the life she suspected he'd lived, yet she still didn't know anything about him. She allowed the sweetness of the moment to bloom for a few minutes as she played.

She happened to glance up at the family picture above the piano. She tried to imagine Frank, or anyone else in the picture. The image would not materialize. No. She'd had enough. Her life was full, and her mission to create a different environment and future fueled and motivated her every day. She had her own business, and the love of family and friends. Complete. The word settled on her like skin.

She wept at the knowledge that she'd come to a place where she was truly happy and content. Struggles were always part of life, and she always had to lean heavily on her heavenly Father to keep going down the path she'd created for herself. It was silly to have entertained a romance even for a few minutes, after all he was just a boy, but she was a woman after all.

CHAPTER 15

Henson walked across the street from the saloon and joined Annie on the veranda.

"Does your wife know you frequent that place?" Annie met his gaze.

"I go in the early part of the evening, before the fellows start getting drunk," he said.

"That doesn't answer my question." Annie shook her head and frowned.

"I'm afraid you may have some trouble tonight, Annie. Ben Suttler is in town. He's brought another load of gold from the mountains, and he's buying drinks for everyone."

"I may have to start locking the front door at 11:00 PM. When he's here, they sometimes celebrate for days on end. It never ends well; someone always gets hurt." The view would be more peaceful on the back porch. Annie stood. "Let's go inside. I'll pour you some coffee."

Henson stood and opened the front door for her.

"Why don't you go and sit on the back porch. I'll bring the coffee out there."

He nodded and made his way out the dining room door to the back porch.

Annie went into the kitchen to get the cups. She

joined Henson on the back porch. The mesquite branches swayed in a soft breeze, and the sky made the perfect backdrop for the mesas in the southern distance. Annie never tired of watching the subtle changes of light and shadow as the mesa swept up to the cap.

"Every time Ben Suttler comes to town, the men in Fort Stockton get gold fever. They are always glad to drink his whiskey, but when he won't share the location of his mine, the tide turns. They fight and carry on. They break all my posted rules after a three-day tear. It's a nuisance." Annie watched a rabbit dart from one bush to another on the side of Callie's shack.

"The only person who benefits is Charlie selling his liquor to a full house for three days straight. Ben runs out of money quick, and then makes another trip to the mountains," Henson said.

"Has anyone ever followed him up there? Checked it out for themselves?" Annie wondered if Ben's wife and children ever benefited from his trips to the mountains.

"I've heard a few tried, but Ben seems to be a master of illusion. But not many risk it, because the Apache still pose a threat up there. It's quite the story that Ben has never had any trouble with them. But it's a fool's wish. There's no gold up there. I believe he helped rob the stage back in the days when it still ran between San Antonio and Pecos, and has hidden a trunk of gold up there somewhere. The Overland stage was robbed on that route several times. When he runs out of money he loads up and heads for the

Guadalupe. Yet he is only gone a few days. He's not mining anything, just retrieving from a stolen cache. I'd bet money on it." Henson stretched his legs, resting his boots on the heels.

"Likely, that's what Barney assumed, anyway. Regardless, Junior can talk of nothing else when Mr. Suttler is here. He's at that age where he can work like a horse, but he's too young to go on adventures. He's never forgiven me for not letting him go on the drive with Jack."

"Junior has had a rough time. He may be only twelve, Annie, but he's weathered more than many men. I just hope he can keep his inner thoughts away from hatred and bitterness. Forgive me for being so bold."

"No, you're right. There are many reasons for Junior to be proud of his father, and many reasons not to be. He's very defensive when he hears bad things about Barney. I'm afraid he will try and identify with the bad side." Annie crossed her arms.

"You know Barney was only that way when he was drinking. If you can impress that upon Junior, maybe it will turn out all right," Henson encouraged her.

"It's my daily prayer. I'll be glad when Jack gets back. I think Junior misses him."

"Add that to your prayers, Annie," Henson said. "Maybe I could take him hunting sometime."

Annie smiled. "That would be nice. He'll have no lack of fun when Jack gets back. His tales will only fuel his discontent, but he'll be old enough to go in a few years."

"I expect so, although I think the cattle will be transported by railway before too long." Henson drained his coffee cup.

Annie shook her head in frustration. "Talk, talk, talk."

"It's bound to come, Annie."

"We'll see," she said and leaned back in her chair.

Even though they sat on the back porch of the hotel, the riotous behavior at the saloon across the street became audible.

Annie stood. "I better see to dinner. At least some of my guests and my family must subsist on real food, not just whiskey. Thank you, Henson, for sitting a bit with me. You're a good friend."

Henson winked. "I believe I'll sit out here a while longer. Just one more day and I can get home to my wife for three wonderful days." He leaned forward and clasped his hands together, tucking his boots underneath the chair.

Annie went inside and started dinner. There were still plenty of beans and bread. She'd fry some chicken and cube some potatoes to roast. The tricky part was not cooking too much while some of her guests reveled in free drinks. She got paid whether they ate or not, but she hated to waste food.

Later Maddie brought Gene and Mavis in to eat.

Frank came in from the back after his trip to the freight station. "No mail for the hotel today, Mrs. Riggs."

No news is good news. "Where's Junior?

Everything's ready."

Maddie looked puzzled. "He's not with you? He didn't come with Mavis after school. I thought he'd come here to help you with something. He does that sometimes, Ma."

"Yes, he does, but I haven't seen him since lunch." She was about to look for him around the hotel when a very drunk Ben Suttler staggered in the front door.

"I want a meal, Mrs. Riggs," he said, nearly falling as he headed for the dining room. He caught himself on the register counter, and then weaved his way into the dining room.

"The sign in the foyer says, 'drinking and boisterous behavior strictly forbidden'." She crossed her arms and gave him a determined look.

Henson must have heard from the back porch since the door was open. He came inside. "Come on, Ben, you don't want to disturb Mrs. Riggs and her guests." He tried to lead him back to the front door.

"I want food for me and my friends!" he shouted. He threw a small, opened draw-string leather bag on her dining room table, small gold nuggets spilling out.

"Gold, Ma, just look at it shine!" Mavis exclaimed. She reached across the table to grab a handful, but Maddie slapped her hand and pulled her back to her seat.

Ben put his hand on his gun.

Annie put her hand in her pocket. They stared each other down, except that Ben was not steady on his feet. Annie thought he might keel over any minute if she could just keep his gaze long enough.

"Now, there's no need for any trouble. I have an idea. Why don't we bring some food for you and your friends over to the saloon. Go on back over there, and we'll be along directly," Henson said.

"I'll agree to that, and there's the payment on the table." He wiped the spittle from his lips with his gun-free arm.

Did she not have a say in the matter? Why should she cater to the whim of this drunken fool? How could Henson put her in that position? She faced Henson and gave a slight stamp of her foot. "Am I to understand you think we should contribute to that drunken brawl across the street?"

"Better than having it over here." His gaze implored her, and he gave a brief nod toward her children sitting at the table.

"Have it your way, I've got to retrieve my son from whatever distraction he's found to be involved in and get him to his supper." Henson was right, but she wouldn't pretend to be happy about it.

"I know where Junior is, Ma," Mavis said.

"And where might that be?" Annie took off her apron and prepared to look for Junior.

"He said he was gonna go up and find Mr. Sutter's gold, then go find Jack and they would start a gang. He packed a bag and left out right after school."

Annie dropped her apron and covered a gasp with her hands. "That was an hour and a half ago. Which way did he go, child? Why didn't you tell someone?"

"I didn't believe him. He went to the cemetery to say goodbye to Pa, but he does that every day."

"I'll go find him, Mrs. Riggs, don't worry." Frank left immediately out the front door.

Annie went out on the veranda and walked quickly to the east end and called, "Junior! Junior, better quit that nonsense and get home!" Her gaze scanned the east end of the grounds. She repeated the same at the west end.

People standing around at the courthouse looked on in amazement.

She ran around the back of the wrap around porch to the south end of the hotel and yelled at the top of her lungs. She couldn't see him anywhere. Darn that Ben Suttler! Junior was probably hiding over at the saloon all afternoon listening to his lies about his stake. She marched around the front of the hotel and ran straight into Abel Marten.

"What are you hollerin' about Mrs. Riggs, what's wrong?"

She continued down the steps but looked over her shoulder. "I can't find Junior. Would you look around for me?"

"Yes, ma'am."

The saloon seemed to move and vibrate with noise of the party going on inside. She opened the door and walked in, searching everywhere. The men didn't seem to notice at first, but then Charlie pushed through the crowd.

"What are you doing in here, Annie Riggs? You ain't been invited to this here party." He stepped right into her face.

She couldn't help it. She hit him so hard in the face

that he stumbled back a few steps. "Thanks to you and Ben Suttler's nonsense, my boy has run away to look for gold. I can't find my son Junior. Have you seen him in here?"

He didn't answer but shuffled off behind the bar.

"Any of you seen my son, Junior Riggs? He's twelve, fair-haired and about this high." She touched her shoulders.

"Annie, he's not been in here," Percival Kettler said, stepping through the crowd. "I've been here all afternoon."

She clicked her tongue and gave him a look that sent him cowering back to his table, and then she began searching every corner, and under every table. She tried to walk behind the bar, but Charlie wouldn't let her pass.

"He ain't here. Maybe he's doin' what his Pa shoulda done years ago, and that's get away from you!"

Mr. Kettler approached the bar and wedged himself between Annie and Charlie. "That's no way to treat a lady, Charlie Simmons. You calm this place down, or I'll go for the sheriff."

"Huh, I bet," Charlie said.

"I'll get some men together, and we'll look for him. You go on back home. We'll find him, don't worry. He'll turn up no worse for the wear, wanting his dinner. You should wait for him at home." Mr. Kettler took her elbow and escorted her out of the saloon. "You have got more guts than any lawman or outlaw I ever heard of. That was dangerous, Mrs.

Riggs."

Annie ignored him and continued calling. "Junior! Junior!" She met Ben Suttler as she hurried back to the hotel to see if he'd turned up there.

"When am I gonna get my food?" Ben took off his hat, smelled the inside of it, then put it back on.

Slapping Charlie Simmons felt so good, she was tempted to serve Ben the same. "Try the Stockton Hotel, you'll get nothing from me today. When you're sober, come and collect your little bag of gold." She pushed past him and nearly stumbled up the steps. *Calm yourself, Annie.*

Henson and Percival Kettler had gathered a group of men. He was filling them in when she walked into the dining room. "Now the boy says he's hunting gold. I don't know if he's been listening to Ben Suttler, but just in case that's what he has in mind, we'll head in that direction. He's been gone about an hour and a half on foot, so if we saddle up, we can overtake him."

Ebenezer Young took off his hat and scratched his head. "You know people go up into those mountains sometimes and never come back. I hope that boy knows what he's doin'."

Annie stepped into the bundle of men. "He's a child, he doesn't know anything. Please hurry!"

"Yes, of course, Mrs. Riggs." Ebenezer tipped his hat at her.

Henson addressed the men again. "Get your horses, and some water, and meet me here in fifteen minutes."

The men hurried out and fanned in all directions.

Annie tried not to think of the stories she'd heard of men going up into the Guadalupe and getting lost. Well, they'd be found but there'd be no flesh on their bones. She shook her head and tried to get a grip. "Maddie, please feed the children and take them to your house."

Maddie nodded and began fixing plates of food for Gene and Mavis.

Junior had been so fractious lately, and Annie had responded unkindly in her frustration. What if she never saw him again alive? If she could just hold him, she would try and make him understand. *Please, Father God, let him be all right.*

Frank barged in on her thoughts. "Mrs. Riggs?"

Annie rose to face him and grabbed his arms. "Did you find him?"

"I found this at Mr. Riggs's grave," he said, handing her a piece of paper.

Annie grabbed it with both hands.

Pa, I'm gonna make things right so Mama doesn't have to work so hard.

Maddie took the children home.

Callie came into the hotel and sat with Annie in the parlor. She kept offering tea, but Annie would take none.

Where was he? What did he mean by his note? Had she caused this by her firm treatment of late? She derided herself for not being more understanding. If she could just get another chance.

Frank and Abel Marten offered to ride the perimeter of Fort Stockton and circle in gradually, covering every area within town.

Henson's group went toward the mountains.

Annie nearly wrung a handkerchief to shreds as she prayed through the night. Her heart sank as the dawn cast a soft light in the rooms.

Bless Maddie, she came early to cook breakfast for the hotel guests. "I took the children to Doña Piña. Mother, Callie and I will strip the beds and make them up again with the spare sheets."

She nodded her thanks, but work would occupy her mind. She prayed again for Junior, and then went into the kitchen to help Maddie. The smell of eggs cooking made her nauseous. Would this nightmare ever end? They worked through the day.

A steady stream of people inquiring about Junior kept the foyer and parlor a busy place.

Right after school, Peck Jones and Josey Flint, Junior's school pals, asked to see Mrs. Riggs.

"Is he lost up there in those mountains, Mrs. Riggs?" Peck's head hung low.

"I'm hoping and praying not. Did he say anything to you two about hunting up gold?" Why hadn't she thought to ask his friends?

"He talked about it all the time, but I never thunk he'd actually do it." Josey looked down as well, and slid one foot back and forth. His blue eyes were filled with regret. "Our mamas won't let us go lookin' for him."

"I should say not. Thanks for your concern boys. I'm sure he'll be found. I'm praying he'll be with you in school come Monday morning." *If I ever let him out of my sight again.*

"Yes, Mrs. Riggs."

Maddie led the boys back outside.

Another long night of anguish kept Annie at her wit's end. Shouldn't there be some word by now? Just as the sun came up Sunday morning, she heard the shuffling of feet at the front door, and the sound of voices. She pulled her keys from her apron pocket and unlocked the door. She'd never seen Henson look so bedraggled. In fact, his entire group of men looked well-worn and exhausted. They held their hats in their hands. She tried not to think the worst.

"We could not find him, Annie. But that's a vast area, and the boy is not an experienced explorer. We'll rest a bit, retool, and head out again in a few hours."

Her heart sank. She willed her legs to remain upright, and tears stung her eyes. She could only nod. "Come in, and I'll warm up some food for you. You can all wash up by the pump out back."

As soon as the men filed through the foyer and out the back door, she dropped to her knees, her head in her hands. The sobs would not come, but a burning pain in her chest nearly choked her. She could not even pray. Somewhere she found the steel that would get her off the floor and into the kitchen.

The men returned to the dining room and sat around the table. Their discussion sounded as if it was under water. Her head ached. Frank and Abel came in with the same report. Dizzyness overcame her, but she forced herself to remain calm. Outwardly, anyway. Within, she suffered.

Doña Piña paid her a visit and prayed a blessing over her and over Junior. She insisted she must not give up hope.

Annie had no plans to give up, but what was her child going through out there in the desert?

The men ate and promised to resume the search shortly. They just needed a rest.

Henson left before the others to see if he could find more help, and Frank and Abel went with him.

When she was alone in the kitchen again, Annie allowed some tears. It made her feel a little stronger, so she set her mind to cleaning the kitchen.

Bare feet ran across the floor in the hotel foyer.

Peck and Josey barreled into the kitchen.

"Mrs. Riggs, we was playin' in the old guardhouse at the Fort, and somebody is banging from underneath the floor. We can't git the trap door open. Do you think it's Junior?" Peck was breathless as he relayed the information.

The chair she sat in nearly turned over as she flew to a stand. Without a word she ran out the door and all the way down the hill. She rounded the curve at Kettler's store and nearly tripped. A few blocks more and she'd be at the guardhouse. Could she lift the trap door? She realized that Peck and Josey were at her heels. "Boys! Find someone to help me," she called over her shoulder. She didn't wait for an answer.

She pulled back the heavy iron gate at the stone building and jumped over the threshold. Her heart pounded in her ears. She dropped to her knees at the trap door and listened. Directly she heard it.

Something was banging on the other side. "Junior! I'll get you out!" She stood up, bent over, and pulled on the iron ring with all her heart. It wouldn't budge. She tried again, and the strain caused her head to pound. Once more she bent, grasped the ring, and pulled with all her might. It opened just a crack.

"Ma!"

Annie fell backwards as the heavy door slipped from her hands. She went to the entrance and screamed for help.

Peck and Josey were running towards her with two Mexican men, employees of Mr. Kettler.

"Please! I can't lift it."

Andres Rivera searched around the jail. He found an iron rod leaned up against the wall. "Mrs. Riggs, as soon as Pedro and I lift the trap, please shove this iron bar underneath, all the way across the top." He handed her the rod.

She nodded and braced herself. Andres and Pedro both took hold of the ring and counted off three. They were able to raise it about three inches and hold it. Annie slid the rod underneath. The men dropped the door.

"We need another man now," Pedro said. Both men clutched their backs and winced from the strain.

Annie knelt and put her face to the opening. "Junior, are you all right?"

"Yes, ma'am, I think so. I'm hungry, though."

"Hold on, we'll get you out."

Henson and Frank appeared at the entrance. "We heard the boys hollering for help. Is he down there?"

"Yes, please help raise the door so we can get him out."

Andres, Pedro, Frank, and Henson bent and slid their hands under the raised door.

"On three," Andres said.

"One, two, three!" They shouted in unison and groaned as they lifted the iron door completely off. They moved it aside to make a hole big enough to retrieve Junior, and then dropped it.

Annie reached down into the cavernous tunnel, as did Frank. They pulled him out of the hole. Annie looked him over from head to toe, front and back and then threw her arms around him. She wept, and she could not stop it.

"I'm sorry, Ma. I'm real sorry. I thought there might be some gold down there, and I wanted to get it. I want to make you not have to work so hard and be like the other ladies. Pa would have wanted that."

She could not speak, but just wiped the dirt from his face with the bottom of her skirt.

"How in the world did you ever get down there? It took four men to get that door open." Henson shook his head.

"I went in through the old hospital. There's just a door and some stairs on that end. But when I started hammering at the walls with my pick, it caved in on that end."

"I don't understand, son. What made you think there was gold down there? It's just a tunnel from the guardhouse to the hospital. When the fort was active it was an escape route in case of attack. It's not a mine shaft." Annie nearly smothered him with her embrace.

"Mr. Charlie told me that it was an old mine shaft. He said there were even old prospector's tools down there. And there were. So, when I took the pick and started hammering away, it caved in, and I couldn't see. I felt my way to this end and could see a little bit of light through a crack. I just kept throwing the pickax up and hit the door. I knew somebody would come. Especially Peck and Josey because we always play in here on Sunday afternoons."

"Charlie Simmons told you this?" Annie could barely put words together, the anger exploded in her breast that suddenly.

"Yes ma'am. He said I should come prospecting down here. He told me I should do it because Pa can't take care of you no more. If I could get us rich, then you wouldn't have to work."

Annie pressed her lips together so hard that it hurt. She bit the end of her tongue to keep for screaming. Charlie Simmons wanted to destroy her, and her family? She closed her eyes and willed deep breaths.

"I'm surprised you didn't pass out from dehydration," Frank said.

"I brung water and ham and biscuits. It run out though. I'm sure glad you come." "I'm glad you're all right, young Riggs." Henson held out his hand for a shake. Junior tried to wipe his hands clean on his trousers, but the grime covered him.

Henson leaned down and shook his dirty hand anyway.

"Thank the men, Junior." Annie said. She stood back while all the men, and Peck and Josey shook Junior's hand.

"I want that hole filled, and this gate locked. Children have no business playing in here," Annie said.

"I'll see to it," Henson said.

The weary troupe filed out of the guardhouse and began the walk up the hill back to the hotel.

Henson and Frank talked about how they had to convince some of the search team to return to town. They had been listening to Ben Suttler and wanted to keep looking for his alleged mine.

Annie sighed. At least they left the comfort of their homes and risked their lives looking for Junior. She'd not quibble about gold fever. Besides, they weren't outfitted for an extended search. Men did dangerous things when it came to alcohol, women, and money. At least the men she knew.

"Are you mad, Ma?" Junior whispered.

"We'll talk about it as soon as we get you cleaned up and fed. At bedtime," she said. She stopped and put her hands on his shoulders, and then placed them on his cheeks. "I am more glad than I can say that you are all right, my son, but we do have some things to discuss." She held him tight, right in the middle of the street.

"Please, Ma, not in front of the men." He pulled away from her.

This boy was becoming a man. She'd have to learn to treat him differently, but she couldn't just turn him out into the world to be absorbed by the violence. Somehow, things would change.

A relieved group of friends waited at the hotel, along with Maddie, Gene, and Mavis. When Mavis saw her brother, she hopped down the stairs and threw her arms around him. When she finally let him go, her green printed pinafore was filthy.

Annie let it go. It could be washed. Annie thanked everyone for their concern. "If you wouldn't mind, I'd like to get Junior bathed, fed, and to bed."

"Will you be at school tomorrow, Junior?" Peck asked.

"Yeah, we've got a math test. But you ain't studied cuz you been buried in that mine." Josey snickered.

Annie pointed her fingers at the boys. "It's not a mine, and I will tell your mothers what you've been up to on Sunday afternoons. There will be no more playing at the guardhouse, or anywhere else on that abandoned fort."

"Yes, Mrs. Riggs," they whined in unison. Both boys sauntered down the steps from the veranda, no doubt blaming Junior for the trouble they'd be in.The crowd dispersed, and Annie pointed to the outside pump. "I'll heat some water for a bath. When you're all cleaned up, you can eat."

Junior went out and began sluicing water on himself. "Maddie, I'll be back in half an hour. I have an errand." Annie walked down the street and entered St. Joseph's. It was so quiet that her dropping coins sounded like pots and pans crashing. She lit a candle for Junior and prayed about the conversation they'd have before bed. She knelt at the altar and thanked God for the men who went searching for him and poured out her gratitude that Junior was all right. Fatigue and weakness settled over her. She thought about when the children would blow air into a pig's intestine, and then slowly let the air out. She could feel strength leaving her body. Her anxiety of the past few days caught up with her. She slumped over the altar."Mija, are you unwell?" Doña Piña was suddenly beside her.

"Could I have a glass of water, please? I'm…I'm just tired."

"Si, mija." Her footsteps hurried away, and momentarily she returned with a cup of water. She held the glass and helped Annie drink it. "I heard the boy was found; *gracias a Dios*."

"Yes, thank you for your prayers, and for watching Gene and Mavis. I don't know what I'll do with him. He's still walking in grief and shadows. I think, Doña, my friend, that he is trying to decide which part of his Pa he'll be. I want more than that for him." Annie felt a little stronger."He's carried a burden. Forgive me, but the feeling toward your late husband, as you well know, is either awe and admiration or fear and disdain such as people feel about wolves. I suppose we all have those two sides warring within us, and as the Indians say, you must choose which wolf to feed." She took Annie's hand and led her to a pew where they both sat down."Yes, it's a terrible burden for a child. He seems more affected by it than his siblings." Annie sighed."Until the child learns to manage his "wolves" you must feed the good wolf. Why not compare him to the good things that his father did, the good attitudes and actions. But perhaps search out the qualities that are unique to Junior and blow the embers of good into a flame."

"I think I know what you mean. I've been so busy trying to keep him on the good side that I've only noticed the times he slips. You've given me something to think about. My thanks." Annie stood.

"I see you home, mija?" Doña Piña stood up and smiled at her.

"I've taken up enough of your time. I can get home. I really appreciate your help and your prayers." Annie walked home deep in thought, and took her time. She wanted to be totally calm when she got back to the hotel.

Somewhere a cow lowed in the evening quiet. The light scent of sage curled around her senses. Her gaze turned west where the miracle fire of sunset glowed. Even in this beauty Annie mulled over what to do about Charlie Simmons. Junior could have died down there. "Father, let this anger in me burn off like that stunning sunset you've displayed this evening. When the morning comes, help me know what to do." She turned the corner to advance up the veranda steps, but looked across the street at the Gray Mule.

Charlie stood in the doorway with Frank Hankins. Neither seemed to notice her as she walked by. They were engaged in a heated argument. Frank must be chastising Charlie for putting gold fever into Junior's mind. That was admirable, but she could fight her own battles.

Just as she went up the steps and stepped inside the hotel, she heard Frank say, "All right, I'll do it. Just leave me alone." Now what in the world could that be about? Frank had talked to Charlie several times, and Annie assumed he did odd jobs for him. Perhaps Charlie had another task that was distasteful. Oh, well, not her business.

CHAPTER 16

What sounded like a herd of cattle blasted through Annie's hotel. She was barely up from her chair before Junior, Errol, Mavis, and Gene burst into the kitchen.

"Mama, there's a man gonna show a moving picture show. He's looking for a place to set it up," Junior said. His sandy colored hair stuck out on all sides from running in the wind."Yes, Ma," Mavis caught her breath, "Can he, Ma, can he do it here?" She clapped her hands and jumped up and down.

"What are you talking about, what man?" Annie sat back down and pulled Gene to her. "Calm down, little one." She tried to sit him on her lap.

"I'm too old to sit on your lap Ma," he said, his indignation damping his excitement a bit.

They were growing up too fast. She needed grandbabies to rock and cuddle.

"Maddie is checking him in to the hotel right now. I heard him say he shows moving pictures. He said he's hoping he can show them at the hotel." Junior motioned for Annie to follow him.

She walked into the foyer, the children at her heels.

"Mother, this is Mr. Alfred Abadie. He has booked a room for two weeks," Maddie said.

"Ah, Mrs. Riggs, how nice to meet you. I wonder if I could discuss a proposition with you?" He bowed, and then clicked his heels together.

"Certainly, please, let's go into the parlor. Maddie, please take the children to my rooms."

"Aw, Ma," Junior said. "We want to hear about it."

She gave him the look that showed she meant business.

He rolled his eyes, but he obeyed.

She'd deal with that face later. Errol, Mavis, and Gene followed Maddie without a word, but Annie could tell they were disappointed.

Mr. Abadie was dressed in all black. He wore a French beret, and his overcoat doubled as a suit coat. His bow tie sported a long tail. He waited until she sat down on the settee, and then he sat in the straight back chair opposite her.

"What did you have in mind, Mr. Abadie?" She folded her hands into her lap. Whatever this distraction turned out to be, it was nice to sit and rest a few moments.

"As your enthusiastic children exclaimed in my hearing, I show moving pictures. I am traveling the country introducing these films to significant towns."

"You consider Fort Stockton significant?" Annie's interest perked up at the sound of a kindred spirit.

"Of course, especially since the railroad is coming through town. It will bring more people, and your town will grow. Moving pictures is the newest social event, and I'm offering to feature your hotel in the maiden voyage of the art in your town."

Everyone seemed to believe that the railroad would indeed come through Fort Stockton. Maybe she should pay more heed. "I see, and what would you require of me?"

"Just the use of your foyer and dining room here. We can set up chairs, invite the public. I will give you half of the proceeds."

"And the cost per ticket?"

"A mere five cents. It's a bargain at any price, but to ensure interest, we will set the price low. What do you say?"

"I want to see the films first. If you'd agree to show them to me before we invite people, and I approve them, then I'll allow it." She'd heard stories of some very risqué films. She'd have nothing of that in her hotel. Excitement sizzled in her throat. The idea of something so modern and different in Fort Stockton gave her chills.

"That sounds like a good deal. Would you like to see them this evening?"

"Yes, I'll be done with meals and other chores by 9:00 PM. You can set up in the parlor since it's just the two of us."

"Certainly." He stood. "And now I'll take a rest from my travels. The buckboard is hard on the back, is it not?"

"Yes, it is. Hopefully, the train will have more comfortable accommodations."

"It will indeed. I've ridden on the Orient line; it is quite nice. Good afternoon, Mrs. Riggs."

She just nodded. Her head was filled with dreams

of future Fort Stockton.

~*~

Annie laughed at how quickly she finished her chores after dinner. Her curiosity was at an all-time high. She didn't know if it was the innovation, or just having something different occurring that made her step quick.

Mr. Abadie was setting up his camera in the parlor when she joined him.

"See Mrs. Riggs, the film that was shot is wound into this large disc and stored in this can." He took the film roll out of the round tin. He treated it with such care, Annie wondered if it was truly fragile. "Please take a seat. I removed a photograph from the wall, I hope you don't mind."

"Not at all." She sat in the straight back chair facing the empty wall.

Mr. Abadie blew out the candles in the room, and then started turning a lever on the side of the camera. A picture appeared on the now blank wall.

She read the words.

Thomas A. Edison, Inc. Cameraman A. Abadie Presents, The Great Train Robbery.

"There will be a few shorts before the main feature. The first is, well, here it comes." He continued turning the lever.

The words *A Cattle Drive* appeared on the wall.

Directly she saw cowboys driving a herd across a river. She could almost hear the groan of the black and white cattle as they swam across the water. The men were submerged up to their necks, but all came out safely on the other side. The crack of the silent whip rendered by one of the cowboys kept the cattle in line as they came out of the water. It lasted about two minutes.

The film stopped.

Annie applauded. "How wonderful. I wonder who those cowboys were."

"I don't know their names, but I shot this film in Oklahoma."

"My son, Jack, is on a cattle drive in that direction. I wonder if it could have been them?"

"I can't imagine. Some of them really wanted to see the finished product, but they had to move on, and it takes great care to process the films. Now for the next short."

The next short section of film featured a man and a woman in a train. He was asking her to marry him, but his hat kept getting blown off.

"Why didn't he just shut the window?" Annie asked.

"It wouldn't be very funny if nothing happened, Mrs. Riggs. It's called comedie'."

"I see, well it is rather amusing."

The film stopped and then words for the next feature began rolling across the wall. *The Great Train Robbery.*

As the film progressed, Annie's stomach tightened. Shooting happened around the train, and on the train. She didn't want to give anyone any ideas when the Orient train came through.

"Is there something else?"

"You don't like this one, Mrs. Riggs?" He stopped turning the film.

"I admit it is exciting, but it's not the kind of future I imagine for Fort Stockton when the train comes through. In fact, that's the kind of thing I don't want."

"I understand, but it is the kind of thing that sells movies. But I will change the film. Perhaps another comedy?"

"Please, we could use some mirth around here."

Mr. Abadie set another film on the camera and began turning the handle. The film told the story of a man so engrossed in his book, that he was completely oblivious to everything going on around him. It was called *An Interesting Story*. Some of the things that happened were funny, some dangerous, but the man in the film never looked up.

Annie was engrossed and laughed out loud. Another thing that tickled her funny bone was that the nail on the wall where the picture had been hanging looked like a fly in the film.

"I'm hoping your enjoyment means that we have a deal?" Mr. Abadie said after the film stopped.

Annie stood and offered her hand. They shook on it.

"I can write up the contract tonight, and if you'll sign it in the morning, I will have the advertisements drawn up. Can we plan to show the films this Friday night?"

"Since it's only Monday, I think that's plenty of

time. If my children have anything to do with it, the word will get out without too much of our effort," Annie said.

He broke down the camera. "I wonder," Mr. Abadie began, "is there anyone about who could play the piano to provide some music for the film? I have noticed your beautiful piano, and I have sheet music that goes along well with the stories." He glanced at her piano.

"As a matter of fact, I can play. May I see the music?"

Mr. Abadie took several sheets of music from a bag next to his equipment.

Annie lifted the cover on her piano and set the music on the stand. She began to play through it. Yes, it did seem to fit the scenes. "I'd be glad to do it," Annie said.

"Wonderful, there is an extra bit of money in it for the musician, Mrs. Riggs. This will be a profitable event for you. We should run it several nights. If attendance seems worth it, I might stay longer."

"We shall see. I'll see if I can get my friend, Henson Jamison, to sign the contract for me."

"Why do we need Mr. Jamison? Can't you sign it yourself?" Mr. Abadie looked puzzled.

"I can't buy a piece of property in West Texas without having a man do the signing."

"Ah, that won't be necessary. I will be happy to have the signature of Mrs. Annie Riggs on the contract. Good night, Mrs. Riggs." He tipped his hat to her.

Annie almost floated to her room. She'd give the

children the news in the morning. What a great day. She had taken a few steps forward to the future. A better future.

With the help of Mr. Abadie's advertisements, and the over-the-moon excited children, the news spread like wildfire. People started arriving at the hotel for the films at 7:00 PM. A half hour later, every chair was filled, and they had to turn people away.

"We'll show them again tomorrow, I promise," Annie said, as she shut the door.

Mr. Abadie had set up a screen at the end of the room, rather than on an empty wall. He gave an introduction to which the audience gave enthusiastic applause. He nodded to Annie, and she took her place at the piano.

Frank and Henson had helped Mr. Abadie move the piano to the front of the foyer, so that she could see the action while she played.

The quiet was palpable as the film began. Annie began to play, and in a few minutes the laughter began. She wished she could see their faces, but she had to keep her eyes alternating between the screen and the sheet music. She suddenly realized that she felt included. As nice as people were to her, she sometimes felt on the outside because of her history. She was in her own hotel, enjoying an event with the community. Somehow, her dreams for her family's future, and the future of the town, might come true.

Near the end of the main feature, Annie heard scuffling through the crowd. The film continued, so she kept playing.

A bottle of whiskey came flying from somewhere behind her and smashed to bits against the movie screen; it tore a hole.

A collective gasp rose in the crowd, and Mr. Abadie stopped the film.

Annie turned to see Charlie Simmons standing in the middle of the group.

Henson left his seat and approached him. "All right, Charlie, you're drunk, and you've caused enough trouble today. Come on, I'll walk you back over to the saloon." He took Charlie by the arm.

Charlie wrenched it away. He doubled his fists and shook them at Annie. "How can you entertain after what you did? You murderin', money-hungry–"

Henson pulled him towards the door before another word could escape.

The silence that followed Charlie's exit soon turned to the murmuring and scuffling of the crowd as they stood to leave.

Annie began to play the piano softly, hoping to calm everyone down.

"Are you all right, Mrs. Riggs?" Mr. Abadie asked.

"Yes, give them their money back." She kept playing, the heat rising on her face. Tears made the sheet music swim, but she played on.

"But, surely not, Mrs. Riggs, surely," he began.

"Return their money, Mr. Abadie. I'll see that you are paid what you would have received for this full house tonight. Please, do it now." Could she just step into one of Mr. Abadie's films, a funny one where everyone got along?

Mr. Abadie made his way to the front door. Annie turned to see him handing out coins to everyone as they left. Soon, the room was empty of guests. Only the children and Maddie remained.

"Good night, Mr. Abadie. Maddie, could you see the children to bed?"

Maddie just nodded.

"I hate that Charlie Simmons!" Gene said.

Annie walked over to her son and grasped his shoulders. "No, you mustn't hate him or anyone. He was drunk. I'm sure he'll think better of it in the morning." She kissed each child on the top of the head as Maddie led them through the courtyard to their rooms.

"Shall we try again tomorrow night?" Mr. Abadie asked.

"We'll discuss it in the morning. I'm–" She bit her tongue. She would not cry.

"Of course, good night."

She put the music in the piano bench, cleaned up the whisky mess, and then headed for her room. She mentally chided herself for thinking that anything could ever change. Drink, hatred, violence. Maybe her dream was a pipe dream, and maybe there was nothing that could make it happen. So many prayers and hopes! Her heart sank under the assumption that there were more of Charlie's kind of people in the world than Annie's kind of people.

Would Barney have enjoyed a moving picture? Or would he have ruined it as Charlie did? When would her thoughts stop bringing Barney Riggs into every situation? How could she expect other people to change if she lived in the past as well?

She undressed and buried herself under the blankets. She'd speak to Mr. Abadie after Mass in the morning. He would have to find some other place to show his pictures. Perhaps the Stockton Hotel. Surely if she stayed out of it, it might be a success.

Maybe Fort Stockton had a better chance without her and her history. She took serious thought of moving to New Mexico with Maddie and Beau.

CHAPTER 17

The next morning Annie walked into the dining room to find Frank replacing the tables and chairs. Annie just nodded to him and went into the kitchen to get breakfast started. She heard more chairs scrap the floor as she fried bacon and cracked eggs into her large cast iron skillet.

Frank came into the kitchen and sat down at the table.

"I heard what happened, Mrs. Riggs. I'm sorry I wasn't here to help. I went with Mr. Young to get his horse out of the mud. The horse was bad hurt, we had to shoot him."

Annie didn't turn around. "I'm sorry to hear that."

"If I'd been here I wouldn't have let him in. I'm real sorry about it."

"No one could have prevented it. Everyone's attention was on the moving pictures." She stirred the scrambled eggs.

"Well, if you try again, I'll guard the front door. Mr. Jamison handed Charlie over to the sheriff. He made Charlie spend the night in jail."

"That's a good thing, except it will make Charlie hate me even more." Annie scooped scrambled eggs into a bowl.

"Maybe the sheriff can keep Charlie locked up until after the show," Frank said.

She didn't plan to try again. "I'm going to Mass as soon as I set the food on the sideboard in the dining room. If you insist on not coming with me, I'll ask you to stay here in case the guests need anything."

"Yes, ma'am."

She went to her room and got her shawl and prayer book. He may have felt truly sorry for her, but she just couldn't talk about it anymore.

She walked down the street to St. Joseph's, went inside to the candle alter and knelt. She dropped a few coins in the basket and lit a candle for Charlie.

"Father God, I want to hate him so badly. He represents everything that is wrong with this town. Jealousy, suspicion, anger, selfish grasping for personal gain. I don't understand how someone like Charlie could be given a fresh start after Barney saved his life, and then his prison release, yet still spew so much hatred. I don't mind telling you that I feel discouraged and must ask forgiveness for that. You have blessed me with the miracle of Christ, and with a loving family, and a gainful business. Show me how to live here, how to make it better for my children." She crossed herself and stood. Her heart was not lifted, so when she saw Father Decorme, she avoided him, but turned and left the church.

She passed several women as they came into the church, but they didn't speak to her. She heard them whispering about what had happened the night before. Did they think she was deaf?

When she returned to the hotel, Mr. Abadie was having his breakfast. A few other hotel guests were at the table. She wanted to get it over with so she went into the parlor, hoping he would join her when he finished eating.

A few minutes later he did join her in the parlor, a cup of coffee in each hand. He handed her a cup.

"How kind. That is just what I need at this very moment." She motioned him to sit beside her on the settee.

"I am so sorry for the catastrophe of last night. I should have hired a guard. It's not the first time that ne'er-do-wells have interrupted my performances. Sometimes even men of the cloth, and devout women of the church try to keep the events from happening. Apparently, my art is from the pits of hell." He shook his head with a slight laugh as he took another sip of coffee.

"I am the one who should apologize. I'm afraid I have an idealistic idea of what my town could be but keep getting thrown down in the mud. Charlie Simmons has a personal grudge against me, totally unfounded, mind you, but he hates me, nevertheless. He sees my prosperity as a direct hindrance to his."

"I was informed of the history of your husband. I think it's wonderful that your Barney Riggs single-handedly squashed the Miller Gang. I've heard of their ruthless murdering and harassment of law-abiding citizens. It would make an amazing movie."

Annie gave him the same look she'd given the unruly Junior the day before.

"Of course, no, but I can't guarantee some other film-maker won't try. It's an amazing story."

"Depends on who's telling it. I'm sorry to inform you, Mr. Abadie, but I can't follow through with my contract. I will definitely pay you, so you won't be at a loss."

"But my dear lady, you most certainly can. We will make sure that we are guarded from disasters such as the one that transpired last night. Your city seemed so keen to be involved."

"May I suggest that you approach the owner of the Stockton Hotel? You will attract the same crowd, perhaps even a bigger one. Their dining room is much larger than mine." She set her coffee cup on the side table.

"I have met Chef Fournier." He crossed his arms, threw his nose in the air and sniffed, and then winked at her.

Annie chuckled at his impression of the chef.

"Besides, I was told, Mrs. Riggs, that you are the most forward-thinking person in Fort Stockton. I am encouraged by the fact that you are hoping for a better town, and not just trying to make more money. You signed the contract, not a man. Are you willing to give up on your project, the one with your name on it?" He grasped both hands around the cup.

"You are an unlikely ally, Mr. Abadie. I need to think a minute." She let her mind go back to the morning before when Mr. Abadie set the official contract in front of her. She'd worn her best dress and relished the thought of writing her own name on the line at the bottom of the page. No other name was over it or under it. Just Mrs. Annie Frazer Riggs. The hope she'd prayed for at Mass rose in her heart. "We shall try again, Mr. Abadie. We'll have Henson and my employee, Frank Hankins, maybe even the sheriff, guard the front door." She shook his hand with a vigor.

"And we shall give them a private showing this afternoon, since they will be outside the range of view this evening? Thank you, Mrs. Riggs." Mr. Abadie stood, and went about his business that morning.

Annie lingered in the parlor a few moments to finish her coffee. She then walked to the kitchen, but not before running her hands across the sign inside the front door.

OWNER AND PROPRIETOR ~ MRS. ANNIE RIGGS

CHAPTER 18

"Mama, there's a man in the foyer with a skirt on, and I can see his knees." Mavis pulled on Annie's dress. "You've got to come see."

Annie knew what kind of man wore a skirt, but for all the Irish in west Texas, they rarely wore a kilt. Mr. Gallagher, the town's first founder, had been the first, but there had been others who trickled to town from time to time.

"Ah, Mrs. Riggs, the proprietor, I'm guessing. Handsome woman ye are, handsome. Very nice to meet ye." The kilted man took Annie's hand and bowed. "Seamus O'Conner, at your service."

Mavis was right, you could see his knees. Annie had seen men in kilts before, but their bare legs always made her feel uncomfortable.

"And is this your bairn?"

"Yes, this is Mavis. Very nice to meet you. Will you be needing a room?"

"Yes, and I'm thankin' ye. I'll be here to scout out land for a golf course."

"A what?" Annie had never heard of such.

"Oh, it's all the rage in Ireland, over the pond. It's a game, and women enjoy it as well."

"What kind of game?"

"Well, you have a piece of land and drill holes in it. Then the players try and lob little balls into the holes. It takes quite a bit of skill to get near the little holes from a distance. I'm thinking when the railroad comes through, I'll make a fair profit."

"And why Fort Stockton?" Annie loved her home, but the reasons people were coming to town all hinged on the railroad.

"Word is spreading that this be a beautiful spot, perfectly situated for the raising of bairns, and doing business. This is a fine hotel ye have here, my lady."

"Thank you." Annie smiled at the thought that Fort Stockton's prospects seem to be improving. "I'll show you to your room." The businessmen may have left her out of the planning, but the hotel would benefit from the railroad. She showed Mr. O'Conner to his room and then went into the kitchen.

Frank came into the kitchen holding a little colored boy by his dirty shirt collar. "Mrs. Riggs, this young'un was stealing out of your trash."

The tears on the little fella's dirty face made tracks. He kept trying to pull away from Frank. "I ain't stealed nothin', ma'am, I was just looking for what food mighta dropped. I ain't eat in a long time. Don't know how long. If it's garbage it ain't stealin', is it?"

"You stay right there, boy." Frank let him go.

"Who are you, little man?" Annie walked over and dried his tears with the corner of her apron.

"I's Hezzie. Don' know no other name. Jez Hezzie."

"Where do you live? Who takes care of you?"

"My mammy died on the stage. We was comin' here from Angelo with the freight line. They buried her right there in the desert where we stopped. And when we got here, they put me out." Of all the cruel things to do. If that was true, she had quite a few words for the stationmaster. How could Philomena let that boy wander away from the station alone? "When was that, Hezzie?"

"Don' know. Been sleepin' in a empty rock house down the hill. Maybe a week?" His shoulders slumped.

"The fort. No blanket or anything? You poor child. Frank, fix him a plate from the sideboard." She took Hezzie by the hand and led him outside to the water pump. She stuck his head under it and pumped. He squirmed and hollered, but she wasn't about to let him sit at her table in such a filthy state.

"Do you have any other family?" She handed him a towel.

"Jez me and my mama, far as I know'd." He rubbed his face hard, and then dried off his head and chest.

Annie led him back inside. She had some of Junior's clothes in her room. She helped him into another shirt and pair of pants. The clothes swallowed him whole. She'd find him some better ones as soon as she could. He remained in his bare feet. "How old are you, Hezzie?"

"Mama says I'm seven, this last birthday," he said.

"Where were you going?"

"Mama worked for the Smeagals, and they was movin' to California. I guess they didn't want me after

Mama died."

"I'm sorry, Hezzie. I'm sorry your mother passed away."

His eyes teared up and he started to cry.

Annie wrapped him up in her arms while his little shoulders shook. What in the world would she do with him? She took him back into the dining room, sat him at the table, and handed him a fork. He surprised her by bowing his head and praying over his food out loud. Annie crossed herself, and Frank looked amused.

"Me and Mama is Baptist."

"Frank, would you get Callie for me, please?"

"Yes, ma'am," he replied and left.

"You can stay here for now, Hezzie, but I don't know what we'll do for the long term. If the Smeagals put you out, there's a chance contacting them won't help."

"Didn't even say goodbye, and they wouldn't even let me cry over my mama."Callie and Frank walked into the dining room from the back porch.

"Callie, this is Hezzie. He's been made a citizen of Fort Stockton, not by choice, but here he is anyway."

"Mr. Frank told me about it. You want him to stay with me? I got an extra little cot in my cabin."

"Well, ain't that nice, Hezzie. You got a meal and a nice warm place to stay. You should thank Mrs. Riggs," Franks said.

"Thank you very kindly, Mrs. Riggs," Hezzie said, holding his chest high. He repeated the phrase he'd no doubt heard in the company of the Smeagals. "Thank you very kindly, too," he said to Callie.

"I gave him a good dousing, Callie, but you might want to heat water and give him a bath. He's been on his own for several days now." Annie would take a tin of cookies over to Callie as soon as she cleaned up after supper.

The next morning Callie came over early. She poured a cup of coffee for Annie.

"Fix you one, too, and let's go out to the veranda. Hezzie still asleep?"

Callie nodded, then poured the coffee, and joined Annie as she walked through the hotel to the veranda. They sat in rockers, sipping hot coffee as the sun came up.

"He did sleep, Mrs. Riggs, but he cried too. Poor little thing, losing his ma so sudden like, and then gettin' abandoned that way. I kinda know how he feels." Callie set her coffee cup down on the table beside her.

"Yes, you do. Maybe you can do each other some good. I'm not asking you to mother him, but there really isn't anything we can do with him. Someone might hire him for a house boy, but I'd much rather see him raised as a child, not someone's work horse."

"Well, long as he's a good boy, I'll look after him. Won't hurt me none, and it might do him some good." Callie grinned, rare for her.

"Unless you've decided to join Lem's family in Atlanta? Have you made up your mind yet?"

"I know he wants me to go there and take care of his mother, my Lucius's mother, but I'm more leanin' on staying here. This is where I met and loved my

Lucius, and where my baby Lemuel is buried. I don't want to get in nobody's way when they didn't know nothin' about me. If it's all the same to you, I'd like to stay and still be your laundress."

"I'd like you to stay and be my friend, Callie." Annie reached over and squeezed her hand. "That is very good news. I've gotten used to your being here, and since Lem came, you seem to be living more. Before you were just waiting. I know it was a hard pill to swallow, hearing that Lucius is never coming back, but if you'll stay with me, I'll see to it that you always have a job. Maybe Hezzie will be a comfort to you."

"We'll see. Thank you, Mrs. Riggs. I'll always be grateful for all you've done. You didn't have to take me in when Lucius left, but you did."

"Please, just call me Annie."

~*~

The day before Thanksgiving, Frank had volunteered to shoot an extra turkey. Annie had commented she wasn't sure that what she had would be enough.

"How'd you manage to get yourself born during Thanksgiving? Double celebrations," Frank said. He set the turkey he'd shot that morning on the kitchen table, already processed. He felt satisfied that she completely trusted him. She'd loaned him a rifle to shoot the turkey, which he set against the wall next to the kitchen table. He could accomplish his goal any time, but with each passing day, he didn't trust himself. Charlie harrassed him every day. With no chance of getting his land, Charlie was determined that Annie had to die. Frank's determination wavered, and it made his stomach queasy."

Actually, there's usually so much going on with this big family, plus the hotel, that sometimes it goes unnoticed." Annie pumped water into a pan, and then washed her hands. She faced him. "Thanks for getting the extra turkey. You'd think four would be enough, but we never know who will show up on the day. Sometimes the cowboys and sheep men do their own thing over an open fire. Not together, of course." She shook her head. "Seems like they enjoy the rivalry between them. But if they don't bring their fights in here, I'm happy."

"So, I guess you'd never bake your own birthday cake, then." He noticed a pan of onions and a knife sitting on the table next to a thick wooden cutting board. He sat down and picked up the knife. "Slices, or chopped?"

"Chopped will be fine. Need them for the dressing. Oh, would you go and gather some eggs? I need to get them boiling." Annie culled through her spices above the sink. "I hope the freight wagons come soon. I'm about out of everything, and so are Kettler's and Young's."

He stood.

"No, I'll get them, you go ahead with the onions. I'll give myself the birthday present of not having my hands smell like onions all weekend." She laughed and walked outside to the courtyard. She spanned the length and disappeared

He wanted to tell her that it was his ma's birthday too, same exact day. November twenty-fourth. But too much talk about his life in Yuma might arouse suspicions, and questions. He'd been amazed that Annie hadn't asked him any questions or didn't pursue information. He chopped onions but his mind went to Ma, no matter how hard he tried to push it away.

~*~

Frankie swept the laundry shack, watching Sissy out of the corner of his eye. Would she laugh at him? "Miss Sissy, what does it take to bake a cake? Tomorrow is Ma's birthday, and I want to make her a party. Just her and me."

"Let's see now, you need flour, baking powder, salt, and sugar for the basics. Depends on what kind of cake you want to make. You got those things at your cabin?" She labored the iron back and forth on a prison guard's uniform.

"How much you reckon all that would cost?" He swept harder. Maybe getting a cake for Ma would be harder than he thought.

"Boy, you ain't got no money." She sat the iron down and fisted her hands on her hips.

"I know, but I want Ma to have a birthday cake. Maybe the baker would give me a job and let me take a cake as payment?"

Sissy stroked her chin. "Hmm, he's not a bad sort of man. Why don't you finish sweeping up and run over there. Ask him real nice if you can do a job for a small cake."

He ran like the wind down the street, pushed open the

bakery door, tripped on the threshold and fell on the floor. He stood up, brushed his pants off, and hoped no one had seen him. No such luck.

The baker's wife was behind the glass counter, wiping it with a cloth. "What do you want? We don't 'llow no beggars in here." She walked around the counter and stood by the open door, her hand pointing for him to leave.

Frankie stood to his full height. "I'm not begging, Mrs. Schmidt. I'm looking for a job."

A boy about his age walked into the room from the back.

Frankie nearly laughed at his suit with the knickers well above his knees. The fabric was blue, and he had a blue silk tie wrapped around his neck tied into a perfect bow. The boy wore a tam, or at least Frankie thought that's what it was called. He thought only girls wore tams. He'd better keep his laughter for another time if he wanted to get a cake for Ma.

"What's he want, Mother?" the boy asked, looking Frankie up and down.

"He wants a job." Mother and son looked at each other and laughed as if it was the best joke they'd heard.

"You can't do nothin'," the boy said. He pulled a stick of candy out of his pants pocket and started sucking on it.

"Yes I can. I can sweep and carry out garbage. I can do lots of things." He looked away from the boy and addressed his mother. "Please, ma'am, I don't even want any money. I just want a cake for my ma's birthday. It doesn't even have to be a big one, just enough for two, or even just one. I'll do anything." Frankie looked around, willing Mr. Schmidt to come through the door. Sissy said he was nice. Wish she'd mentioned the missus and her girly son.

"Ain't that sweet, he wants a cake for his ma. Don't

you got nobody to cook you a cake?" the boy asked, crunching a bite of his candy, and talking with his mouth full.

"I ain't got no need of any help. You can buy a cake, like everyone else. Who's your ma, anyway?" Mrs. Schmidt screwed up her nose, as if she smelled something awful.

"Elizabeth Jennings is my ma. Tomorrow's her birthday. She's a Thanksgiving baby," Frankie said. He was proud of the fact that his ma was born on a national holiday. President Lincoln made it so.

"Elizabeth Jennings?" Mrs. Schmidt's face flashed red in an instant. She doubled up her fists.

Frankie thought she would hit him.

"Get out, you miserable cur." She grabbed him by the shoulder and threw him out.

He landed in the dirt. He sat up and shook his head. His lip bled. He looked up to the bakery window, and little boy blue was staring at his mother with wide eyes, candy stick hanging out one side of his mouth. Frankie picked himself up and walked back to Sissy's laundry shack.

"Well, what did he say? Did he give you a job in exchange for a cake?" Sissy asked, looking up from her laundry. "Law! What happened to you?"

"He wasn't there, and Mrs. Schmidt threw me out. She got real mad when I told her who my ma is. Why would that make her so mad?" He rubbed his sore lip.

"Oh, shoot a mile. I forgot to tell you not to mention your name, or especially hers." She slammed the iron down on the table.

"But why? Why would that make her so mad?" Frankie joined her at the table.

"Oh, well, Mr. Schmidt frequents the saloon where your ma works. She probably thinks her husband spends too much time there." Sissy coughed, and then stood and resumed her ironing.

"Well, it ain't Ma's fault. I won't be gettin' a cake for her birthday tomorrow." Frankie tried not to cry. He wanted to make her feel better about baby Clyde. They both missed him so much.

"Hmm, well, it ain't over yet. I might just run into Mr. Schmidt before tomorrow, and well, just you go on home, and leave it to Sissy." She grinned at him.

The next day, Ma's birthday was almost over before he heard a knock on the door. Sissy must have come through! He ran to the door to meet her so maybe Ma wouldn't hear. He wanted it to be a surprise. She was out back getting her stockings off the clothesline.

He threw open the door, but it wasn't Sissy. Mrs. Schmidt stood in the doorway holding a beautiful cake. It was the prettiest thing Frankie had ever seen. Had Sissy made her change her mind? It was unbelievable that the baker's wife brought it all the way out to their cabin from town.

"Come in, Mrs. Schmidt." Frankie opened the door all the way, careful to avoid her free hand.

"Where's your ma?" Mrs. Schmidt looked around the cabin with an expression as though she'd stepped in a cow patty.

Frankie had cleaned the house for ma and put a bowl of persimmons on the table. Sissy had given them to him. Ma had said they was pretty. He was proud for Mrs. Schmidt to see the cabin all spiffed up. "That's a pretty cake. I can sure come and do some work for you to pay for it."

Frankie remembered what Sissy had said about Mr. Schmidt going to the saloon where Ma worked. This looked like a charitable visit, but just in case, he said, "You can just leave it if you want. I'm sure you have things to do to get your Thanksgiving all ready for Mr. Schmidt and, what was his name, your boy?" Frankie couldn't take his eyes off that cake. It looked all plummy with white icing. And there was more than enough for a few days.

"His name is Percy, and I'll just give it to her in person."

Frankie closed the door and stood with his hands behind his back. "She'll be here directly, she's just gettin' the wash off the line. Won't you sit down?" He'd heard Sissy say that when a friend of her ma's visited the shack one day.

"I'll stand, if you please."

Ma walked into the room from the back door just then. "What's this?" Her face went white.

"Mrs. Schmidt brought you a birthday cake, ain't that nice?" Frankie went to her and pulled her farther into the room. He hoped the baker planned to let him work it off, because if Mrs. Schmidt asked for money, there wasn't any.

Ma's face scrunched into a ball of confusion. "I don't understand?" She crossed her arms and pulled Frankie behind her.

"Your boy came in begging for a cake for your birthday," she said. She lowered her head, and her eyes grew dark.

Frankie stepped from behind Ma. "I didn't beg, Ma. I asked for a job."

"Why don't we sing and congratulate her on her

birthday," Mrs. Schmidt said. She began singing, "For she's a jolly good fellow, for she's a jolly good fellow."

Frankie joined in for the last, "For she's a jolly good fellow, which nobody can deny."

As they finished, Frankie couldn't understand why Ma wasn't smiling.

Mrs. Schmidt stepped forward with the cake in her hands. She turned it sideways and smashed it into Ma's face. "Happy Birthday, Mrs. Jennings. Stay away from my husband!" She turned and stomped her way out the front door, slamming it behind her.

Frankie's breath caught in his throat. Tears stung his eyes.

His ma was covered with cake all over her face, neck and the top of her dress. She wiped cake out of her eyes.

He thought she'd cry, but she just shook her head. She grasped a handful of cake and offered it to Frankie, and then she gave herself a bite. "Not bad, at least she didn't skimp on the sugar for a cake she meant to destroy," Ma said.

Frankie just stared at her.

"I have to go change for work, you don't mind cleaning this up, do you? Salvage what you can." She stood and went to her bed, and pulled the quilt closed so she could dress.

"Ma, I don't understand. Why would she do that?" Frankie bent to pick up chunks of smashed cake.

"Oh, never you mind. She's just mean. She's not the only wife in Yuma that would like to smash my face."

"Because you're prettier than them? Cuz you are, Ma."

She poked her head out from behind the quilt. "Well, happy birthday to me. That's awful sweet, Frankie. Now clean this up, and don't be worryin' your head about why people don't like me. I, for one, don't care no more." She hummed as she finished dressing.

Frankie hoped he'd understand things better when he got older. But he had to admit. Ma may not care what people think, but he sure did. He cared what they thought about her.

~*~

Frank shook the memory from his head.

Maddie walked into the kitchen, her arms full of a giant pumpkin. "Hi, Frank. Ma got you choppin' onions, I see." She set the pumpkin on the table.

"I volunteered. She wanted a birthday without her hands smelling like onions." He chopped away.

"Birthday! Oh, law, I nearly forgot. With all the Thanksgiving preparations, and the children being sick, I didn't even think about it."

"I have an idea. Why don't we do something for her birthday? Maybe take her to the Stockton Hotel for dinner. I've saved my wages, I think I can afford for us to all go together." He smiled, thinking of his own ma. How she would have loved a special day like that. But since that day with Mrs. Schmidt, he'd never liked cake that much. Mrs. Riggs could have cake if she wanted it.

"That sounds like a splendid idea, but let's keep it a secret. Let's get through Thanksgiving with her thinking we all forgot. Then Friday we'll all take her to the Stockton. She'll not have to cook that day, I'll take care of that, and she can wear her new hat that Beau sent her from New Mexico." Her eyes shone with excitement. "Brilliant, Frank. You seem to be such a big part of this family, it's almost as if you were always here. I can't tell you how much your help has meant around here." She patted him on the shoulder.

Frank looked down. Guilt constricted his throat. "Yes, ma'am," he said. Suddenly, he remembered why he was in Fort Stockton, and what he'd vowed to do.

"Aw, don't be shy. You're a hard worker. But I'll tell you, it will take all of us chipping in for that meal at the hotel, but we'll all contribute. Good thinking, Frank."

He chopped more onions, glad that they made his eyes water. He could get away with the emotion that choked him without Maddie being the wiser. Could he kill Mrs. Riggs? What would his ma say if he came home without having done it?

He decided then and there. He would tell Charlie that the murder of Mrs. Barney Riggs was not going to happen. He changed his mind. Annie Riggs had nothing to do with what happened to his family. It was all Barney Riggs's doing. He'd not make Annie and her family pay for it. He'd leave as soon as he could, but not before telling her the truth. Mrs. Riggs needed to watch out for Charlie Simmons, and also for strangers who happened into town. Could it be he was the only one seeking revenge?

For now, he'd put it out of his mind and do all he could to help her.

CHAPTER 19

Annie stretched her legs at the piano. It had been a rare treat for Maddie and Mary to offer to do the cooking that day. She must have looked tired after serving all the guests for Thanksgiving, and then helping with their own family meal as well. She'd been given a day off and she didn't quite know what to do.

Doña Piña had taken the young children for the day, and Sarah had offered to strip the beds with Callie.

She'd played all the piano music hiding away in her bench, and then played around with some tunes of her own.

"Mother, why don't you put on your best dress and your new hat. One of the guests is a photographer, and he offered to take some photographs of the family. We haven't done that since, well, a long time ago." Maddie had a strange wiggle in her smile.

"Well, how much will that cost me?" Annie asked with a chuckle. The last time they'd sat for a family photo was when she was still married to James. Why hadn't they ever sat for one with Barney and his children?

"Oh, Beau will pay for it. Just you get dressed and meet us on the veranda," Maddie said and left the parlor before Annie could protest. It had been nice having Beau home for Thanksgiving. He hoped to be able to bring Maddie and the children to New Mexico soon.

She did want a new photo with the family, plus she wanted a picture of the hotel with the Riggs sign on it. She went to her room and dressed.

She'd been wondering about Frank. He'd been scarce on Thanksgiving Day, after working like a slave on the day before. Maybe he had his meal with some of the cowboys. She'd decided to ask him about his family, to find out just where he was from and what he planned to do.

She finished dressing and walked through the hotel to the veranda.

"Oh, my goodness, what is this?" She reached out her arms to embrace her grandchildren, who were running up the steps to meet her.

"It's a surprise, Ma," Gene said. "We takin' you to the fancy hotel to eat dinner. All of us is going." Gene held her hand and pulled her down the steps.

Frank drove up with Biscuit attached to the carriage. He took off his hat.

Maddie and Beau drove up behind him in their buckboard.

"Happy Birthday, Mrs. Riggs." Frank grinned, and then jumped down. He stood at the carriage and helped her up, and then her sister.

The children rode with Maddie and Beau.

"Well, isn't this a nice surprise," she wondered aloud. She'd been dying to see inside that hotel, and now was her chance. Just what was on that menu that made Chef Fournier's food better than hers? Well, at least he couldn't hold a candle to her biscuits.

The children sang nursery rhymes and the mothers clapped.

Ten minutes later, they pulled up into the yard of the Stockton Hotel.

Frank and Beau helped everyone out of the wagons.

They walked inside and the first thing that Annie noticed were the crystal chandeliers. They sparkled in the candlelight. Each round table had a white tablecloth, a lit candle, and a little spray of leaves and blooms. There must have been ten large round tables with eight chairs each.

"Welcome to the Stockton Hotel. I'm your maitre'd, Henri Dubois. Please, if you'll wait, we'll join some tables so that your party can sit together."

Annie nodded. Where did Henry Delbert get off calling himself Henri Dubois? She couldn't stifle a laugh. No doubt at the orders of Chef Fournier.

Directly they were seated.

Chef Fournier came out of the kitchen and walked over to their tables. "Mrs. Riggs, what a nice surprise. I wondered when your curiosity would get the better of you." He twirled his little curly mustache.

"Not curious at all, Chef Fournier. I have been gifted this outing for my birthday, and to make it special, I think my family thought it best to have it somewhere else besides my hotel, where my responsibilities are always present." She noticed the cooks watching out the double-door windows of the kitchen.

"Could we see a menu, please?" Maddie asked.

"Oh, my dear," Chef Fournier said, "The special today is succulent baked chicken with jalepeno pear sauce, a side of roasted potatoes, and..."

"Thank you, Chef, but we'd like to see a menu," Annie said. She bit the end of her tongue to keep from laughing. Did he think the menu would reveal secrets?

"Of course." He walked away, but not before signaling Henry with the snap of his fingers.

Henry nodded, picked up a stack of menus and brought them to the table. He gave one to each adult.

Annie opened the menu and scanned it. All the offerings were in French, with the translation below. Mostly different versions of ham, fowl, and multiple ways of prepared potatoes. The dessert menu consisted of several flambe' selections. The last section on the menu touted *Special Offerings*.

Among the list of drinks and desserts was listed "Pastry Deluxe, Recipe courtesy of the Riggs Hotel."

Annie nearly choked on the sip of water she'd just taken.

"Ma!" Maddie whispered. Did you see?"

"Yes, Daughter, I saw it."

"Did you give him our family biscuit recipe?"

"Of course not. I'm sure it's his own recipe that he's attributed to me. I know he never thought I'd ever set foot in this place." She kept her composure. "Don't let him know we've seen it. And for goodness sake, everyone be sure and order them." She didn't know whether to be offended or flattered. It's a wonder the news hadn't gotten to her before now. He'd outright misrepresented himself. She'd at least have a little fun with him and be grateful for the free advertising.

A cold thought crept up her back. What if the biscuits weren't good? What if he meant it to ruin her?

The waiter returned to the tables.

"Ma, you order first, this is your night." Maddie said.

Everyone clapped for her.

"Thank you." She turned to Henry. "I'll have the special that Chef Fournier mentioned, and a side of Pastry Deluxe." She, showed him the menu with her finger on the word "Riggs".

"Of course, madam." He didn't flinch or look worried. He took everyone else's order and left the table. Half an hour later, the meals arrived, accompanied by Chef Fournier. "I must apologize to you Mrs. Riggs, and to your guests. It seems you all ordered the pastry, and I'm afraid we are all out. It's our most popular item," he said, eyeing Annie for a response."Not even one? I was so looking forward to eating a biscuit that I didn't have to cook."

"Ah, merci, I'm sure, but I'm afraid it's out of the question."

"We're not in any hurry there, pardner. If you want to mix up a batch, we can wait," Frank said.

Chef Fournier gulped. He looked as if he stood on a horse with a rope around his neck, and someone was about to slap the horse on its haunches.

"Maybe next time, then. This all looks delicious."

Annie gave an eye to the family. That was to be the end of it. Chef Fournier hadn't done her right, but she'd deal with it her own way, and not by humiliating him. Besides, The Stockton was just as important to the railroad coming through as any of the businesses in town.

Chef Fournier gave her a superficial smile. Surely, he had to wonder when the ax would fall. "Please, enjoy your dinner. And happy birthday, Mrs. Riggs." He sniffed and slung his nose up into the air as he walked back into the kitchen.Annie took a bite of the chicken. Very good. The pepper was just enough to enhance the flavor of the stewed pears, but not too hot. She loved jalepenos, but not when they were so hot that she couldn't taste her food.

The potatoes were done to a turn. The beans were white, and lightly seasoned. Navy beans, she assumed. The family seemed to be enjoying their meal. This was a sweet treat. It wouldn't do to get used to it. There would never be any end to the work, but thankfully, she loved it. Still, it was rare and appreciated to have a break, and to be treated out to dinner.

Everyone finished eating except Gene, who picked around his chicken. Annie wondered if it was too hot for him. "Gene, just finish your potatoes. I think we'll order dessert."

No sooner had Annie said "dessert" did Chef Fournier walk from the kitchen holding a beautiful cake. It had a delectable white icing and cherries arranged on top. The wait staff and cooks followed behind and they began to sing, "For she's a jolly good fellow..."

Gene stood on his chair and sang louder than anyone.

Junior stood beside his mother, patting her back in time to the music.

"For you Mrs. Riggs, a fresh plum cake." Chef Fournier bowed low, still holding the cake.

Frank left the table.

CHAPTER 20

Annie finished her morning coffee on the veranda but decided to sit a bit longer. She relished the success of the moving picture event from the night before. Either Charlie didn't try to ruin it this time, or Frank and Henson had kept him at bay. This morning she didn't care which. The program seemed to delight a full house. Every chair in the hotel had been occupied, she'd allowed about a dozen to stand.

Her attempt at trying to play the sheet music and match it with the action had been enjoyable, if not totally fitting. The gasps, and "Ahhs" and laughter thrilled her soul. The excited and mirthful chatter after the films finished filled her with joy. To have provided a community event like that made her feel she'd taken a few steps toward her dream of a better future for her community. She leaned back in her rocker, closed her eyes, and smiled.

"Must be a happy dream," a man's voice said.

Annie opened her eyes and felt a warm flush explode on her cheeks.

An elderly, rather portly gentleman in a suit and tie clicked his heels. "Alfred Callaghan, at your service, Ma'am."

"Oh! Excuse me. I'm sorry. Can I help you?"

Annie stood, and the forgotten coffee cup in her lap rattled across the veranda floor.Mr. Callaghan bent to retrieve it for her. "I'm so sorry, I didn't mean to startle you. At least it didn't break." He handed her the cup, and then took off his brown bowler hat.

Annie resisted the urge to reach up and smooth down his gray hair that stuck out on all sides like chicken feathers. "Quite all right, thank you."

"I'm in need of a room, if you have any vacancies," he said. He appeared slightly winded as he dabbed perspiration from his neck and brow with an already very damp handkerchief.

The chilly morning should not have made him so visibly covered with perspiration, but perhaps he'd walked a long way. She didn't see a horse or buggy anywhere. Perhaps he walked from the station.

"Certainly, follow me." Annie turned to walk into the hotel, but he stepped beside her and opened the door with a bow.

Annie stepped around the front desk, and turned the guest register toward him. He grinned at her as he took the plume from its holder and penned his name.

"Normally, Mr. Callaghan, guests have to be prepared to share a room with a stranger. I hope that won't be a problem."

He squinted and cocked his head a bit to the side. "Hmmm. What if I pay double. Could I have the room to myself then?"

"I think that could be arranged, Sir. How many days do you plan to stay?" Annie asked, admiring the flourished signature style of his name on the register.

"Honestly, I'm not sure, but I can certainly pay. In fact, let me pay a week in advance," he said as he retrieved his wallet from a pocket inside his suit coat. He paid her and continued to stand at the counter. "Is there a place I can store my valuables safely?" he asked.

"Yes, normally, but I didn't offer because you have the room to yourself. But of course, I can lock your valuables away, if you like."

"Wonderful." He pulled a long, envelope-sized leather satchel from his coat pocket and handed it to her. He waited as she opened the safe and placed the satchel inside, and then locked it up again. He'd listed his home as Jasper County, Texas.

"You've come a long way, Mr. Callaghan. East Texas must seem like a whole different country than our sparse, arid west."

"Yes, the piney woods are a sight to see, and made me my fortune. I've just sold my sawmill business and decided to travel a bit, see the rest of this vast state of Texas. It is quite humid there, though, and that's a huge difference in the two climates. I find this dry climate much more agreeable, however I do miss the trees and water." He offered nothing more.

"Well, let me show you to your room." Annie gave him the key to his room.

"Splendid. I am rather tuckered out after that walk from the station at the edge of town. Oh, one last question before I retire," he said.

"Yes?" Annie replied.

"Where might one buy a coffin in this town?"

Annie stumbled over an answer. "Well, um, there's a carpenter located behind the livery. You can inquire there." She racked her brain to remember if anyone had recently died. Someone he knew, perhaps? She wouldn't pry.

"Thank you, ma'am. Now, don't trouble yourself. Just point me in the right direction."

"Just through there, across the courtyard, third room on the right." Annie showed him to the side door that led from the dining room to the courtyard.

He tipped his hat at her and stepped toward the courtyard.

That afternoon, as Annie chopped onions for the beef stew she'd planned for supper, she noticed Mr. Callaghan slip out of the hotel. If it weren't for the tears rolling down her cheeks from the onion fumes, she might have called out a greeting.

That evening at supper, Mr. Callaghan held her guests enthralled as he recounted his recent misfortune. "Two wicked ne'er-do-well thieves robbed the post office in Jasper, Texas, which was next door to my office. To cover their crime they set the building on fire. Unfortunately, it burned down nearly the whole town."

"Oh, my. How terrible," Annie said. "Were there any lives lost?"

"Several, including my wife. I was miles away at one of my mills, and she was waiting for me in my office. Millie had fallen asleep on the divan. It can only be surmised that she succumbed to smoke before she could escape."

An uncomfortable silence fell on the room. A few sniffs could be heard among the ladies, and the men shifted in their chairs and coughed.

"I'm so very sorry for your loss," said Annie. She knew his grief first hand.

"That's why I sold out and have traveled this last year. I apologize. I surprise myself when the tale just spills out like that. I've rarely spoken of it." He tapped his fork on the table. "We were not blessed with children, and traveling seemed the only way to fill the void."

"You'll find you're among friends here, Mr. Callaghan. I hope you'll stay in Stockton for a while. We'll show you the beauty of our country. Would you care for another piece of pie?" Annie reached for his plate.

"No thank you, but that was a mighty fine stew. I should turn in. Have to see a man in the morning." He rose and left the table.

Right, the coffin. He'd given no indication who he wanted it for. Again, Annie again decided not to pry.

Mr. Callaghan did not present himself for breakfast the next morning.

Maddie came in early to clean the rooms and help with breakfast. She approached Annie in the kitchen. "Mr. Callaghan is dead, I think."

Annie rushed to his room, and Maddie was right. He was already cold. He must have passed during the night.

"Maddie, go for the sheriff."

How very sad. She knew the sheriff would want

his personal effects so she retrieved them from the safe.

Inside the satchel she'd stored away for him was an envelope that read, *In the Event of my Death.* She felt as though she encroached on something very private, and returned the envelope to the satchel. Frank and Henson, who had come in for breakfast, carried Mr. Callaghan over to the Grey Mule. The back room with its large window, served as a holding spot for corpses until they could be claimed. Sometimes days would pass before a body was claimed and buried. Annie hated walking past there when a delay made the air putrid with decay. The open window, although beneficial for controlling the scent in the saloon, also drew critters of all kinds. She hated the thought of poor Mr. Callaghan's earthly vessel vulnerable to crows, insects, and worse.

Sheriff Comhars arrived and Annie handed him the envelope Mr. Callaghan had given her for safe keeping.

He pulled out the contents and listed the items out loud. "A wad of cash, and a letter." He unfolded the letter and read it. "Well, he must have known he wasn't long for this world. He left instructions for his body, and anything left to his person, to be shipped to a sister in Boston. He's given the name of a lawyer for his sister to contact for the reading of his will. He assures her that he has left his entire estate to her."

A lump rose in Annie's throat. "He inquired about a coffin yesterday. It never occurred to me that it was for himself. Bless him." She crossed herself.

"Yes, we found a receipt for said coffin in his coat.

I'll check with the carpenter. As soon as he's finished building it, we'll get this poor stranger on the wagon for his long journey north."

Stranger. He hadn't seemed a stranger at dinner the night before. Yet, what did Annie know about him? Only that he seemed unwell, had a terrible tragedy in his recent past, and was a wealthy man.

"He's also left instructions to telegraph a friend of his in east Texas." Sheriff Comhars tucked the money and letter under his arm and started for the door, but stopped short. "What did he owe you, Mrs. Riggs?"

"Oh, nothing, he paid ahead. I'll take care of the telegraph to his friend in east Texas."

"That's kind of you. Here's the name of the friend. A Mr. Leeland Lawless, in Jasper, Texas." He pointed to the name on the instructions. "I don't suppose you could," he began but hesitated.

"I can, Sheriff. I'll sit up with him tonight."

Sheriff Comhars tipped his cowboy hat and left the hotel, his boots clunking across the wooden floor.

She sent the telegram to Mr. Lawless, informing him of Mr. Callaghan's death, and then Annie worked through the afternoon with her usual gusto. Her mind kept taking her to Mr. Callaghan. Yes, he did demonstrate signs of heart disease. That walk from the station didn't help, nor the heavy meal of stew, bread and butter, and peach pie in great quantities. He must have known his time was nigh. What did it feel like to purchase your own coffin?

That evening Frank walked her across the street to the saloon. "Kind of you to sit up with the dead man, but you'll have to walk through the men drinking." He held up the oil lantern as she stepped into the street.

"A temporary discomfort."

As they approached the saloon front door, Frank handed her the lantern. "Well, I'll leave you to your vigil. Miss Maddie has asked me to stay with your children tonight for an hour. She wants to visit a sick friend."

"That's wonderful, Frank. I'll see you tomorrow."

"I'll check on you after my visit at Maddie's. Have everything you need?" Frank asked, poking his hands into his jeans pocket.

"I have my Bible and the lantern to read by. I daren't trouble Charlie for a glass of water, so I've brought my own jar." She pulled it from her apron pocket.

Frank looked down. "Probably a good idea." He turned and went back toward the hotel.

Would she ever figure him out? Gene cared a lot for Frank, and she was glad for them to spend time together.

Annie stepped inside the saloon and a hush fell over the place. She glanced to her right where Charlie stood, drying glasses with a dirty cloth. He glared at her. She felt tempted to reach her hand into her pocket just to give him a start, but thought better of it. The patrons of his establishment were already drunk. It wouldn't take much to start a brawl. Annie thought about the contents of her apron pocket. She relied upon the strength it gave her.

Charlie spit tobacco on the floor, his glance

radiating hate.

She lifted her head and made her way through the men toward the back room. As soon as she closed the door, the din of drunken celebration continued. She turned up the lantern for a brighter glow. A stack of rifles leaned against the wall just inside the door, and a table against the perpendicular wall held a pile of pistols. At least Charlie had the presence of mind to collect their weapons before they began to drink.

Mr. Callaghan lay out on a long table pushed up against the open window. The sheet that covered him was none too clean. She'd go back to the hotel for a clean one if she didn't have to walk back through the saloon. She sighed, crossed herself, and sat down in a straight back chair that flanked the table. She set her jar of water on the floor next to her and set the lantern at Mr. Callaghan's head.

Her fingers found the lace ribbon marking a spot in her prayer book. She opened to that place and began to read. Her mind wandered to the unknown life of the man stretched out before her. She'd listened with great interest of his accounts of the railroad in east Texas. How it made his business soar to new heights, and all the people and efforts that had come there. He and his wife had taken trips that took only a few days over distances that would take weeks by freight. *Oh, if only it would happen for the west!*

Annie heard a rattling and movement outside the window. She often heard the wind rustle the junk in the back of the bar, even from the hotel veranda. She paid no mind to it, except to wish Charlie would clean up his digs. Her thoughts returned to her reverie.

She imagined young Gene, Errol, and Junior, even Mavis, boarding the train for college in the north, and stalwart men of character and means stepping off. Men and women with dreams and visions of a bright future that could provide commerce and progress for Fort Stockton.

Although Belle's tea party accomplished nothing of Annie's hopes, still, perhaps the train would bring forward thinking women to the west. Annie laughed as she realized her fantasy did not show a woman stepping off the train on the arm of a man, but alone and unafraid with her head held high and her own ideas. She propped her elbow on Mr. Callaghan's table and leaned her head against her hand with a sigh. Oh, what she could have learned from Mr. Callaghan, now lost. She could read all day long, but to talk to a person who'd experienced that kind of progress stirred her soul.

A scraping sound outside the window disturbed her thoughts. She turned her head in that direction.

An enormous coyote jumped through the window and landed right on top of Mr. Callaghan. Annie jumped to her feet. The animal growled at her and she froze. It sniffed at Mr. Callaghan's face and it pawed at the sheet.

She could stand there in statue-like fear, and felt she probably should, but with each breath a silent prayer, she slowly, and by half inches, backed toward the door as the beast continued sniffing and pawing at the corpse. Her leg bumped against the stack of rifles.

The sound of it drew the attention of the coyote, and it jerked its head toward her with a seething growl. He reared to pounce as Annie reached behind her, grabbed a rifle, swung it around, cocked the lever and fired. The recoil threw Annie against the door, and she slid to the floor.

The coyote yelped and then slumped off the table, blood smearing the sheet that covered Mr. Callaghan.

Annie's heart pounded. *Thank You, Father God!* She tried to stand up but found her arms and legs failed her, and her hands shook. She tossed the rifle away from her. The door pushed against her back.

"Mrs. Riggs, are you all right?" Frank asked, his tone sounding panicked. The door pushed harder against her back.

Annie scooted away from the door so he could get in. Both he and Henson pushed themselves through the partially open door and helped her to a stand.

"Well, it's obvious what happened. Did it hurt you, Annie?" Henson took his handkerchief from his pants pocket and dried tears she didn't realize she'd begun to shed.

"You're all right, now, Mrs. Riggs. Let's get you home." Frank put her arm around his neck, and his other arm around her waist and began walking her out of the room. He called back to Henson. "I'll come back and sit up with that body the rest of the night, Mr. Jamison. I'll be back as soon as I get her settled."

"All right, and I'll take care of this critter," Henson said.

"How'd ya'll get here so fast?" Annie asked.

"Mr. Jamison met me as I was returning from Maddie's, she wasn't gone that long, and we decided to hang around just in case the crowd got too rowdy and caused you any trouble."

As they walked through the saloon to the stare of drunken cowboys and shepherds, Annie noticed Charlie sitting at a table near the bar. He whistled a merry tune and he did not look up at her. She supposed news of the incident had already made its way to the room, but how? Henson and Frank were the only ones to come to her aid, and there was no one else in the hall. What did it matter? Charlie's hatred of her seemed to know no bounds.

Frank spoke to one of Annie's hotel guests who sat near the door. "Please, could you go for Mrs. Piña and ask her to come to the hotel to help Mrs. Riggs? Her house is in the old sutlery across from the courthouse."

The cowboy nodded, followed them out the door, and headed toward the courthouse.

"Poor Mr. Callaghan," Annie said. She shuddered at the disheveled state of his current place of repose. "Frank, when you return, please take a clean sheet and some rags to clean up the mess."

"Yes, ma'am." He settled her into her rocking chair in the parlor. "Mrs. Piña will be here in a moment to help you to bed." Frank set down in a chair near her. His hands shook.

"My goodness, Frank, are you all right?" Annie reached for his hands to steady them.

"You could have been killed, Mrs. Riggs. In fact, I'm surprised you are untouched, except for being shaken up. Whew!"

"I prayed, and God gave me strength and the presence of mind to use that rifle. Thank heaven it was loaded." Annie squeezed his hands in hers.

"But how did you have time to pray?" Frank looked directly into her eyes.

"It's like breathing, Frank, it's always with me." Annie took a deep breath and with a long exhale, realized how very tired she felt.

The front door opened.

"Mija!" exclaimed Doña Matilde.

"Oh, I'm fine, just a bit kerfuffled. I had a run in with a coyote." Annie yawned.

"She killed it, Mrs. Piña. It was the darndest thing," Frank said.

"Well, let me get you to bed. You look as though you fought and lost," Doña Matilde said with a small laugh.

"Thank you, ma'am. I'm going back over to help Mr. Jamison clean up that coyote mess." He turned to leave.

"Don't forget the rags, and the clean sheet for Mr. Callaghan," Annie called.

Doña Matilde helped her up and they started toward her room.

"Yes, ma'am," Frank replied, and the front door slammed.

~*~

"Look at this," Henson said as Frank walked into

the saloon back room.

The coyote was covered with the dirty sheet that had been on the body. Henson held up Mr. Callaghan's head. "There is a piece of raw meat under his head. As far as I can tell, it's not part of Mr. Callaghan's person. At first I thought the coyote had torn at his neck, but the man's neck is intact." Henson lay the head down, and then wiped his hands with his handkerchief.

Frank lifted his hat and scratched his head. "What could that mean? Is that some sort of local religious ritual or something?"

Henson shook his head. "I think it means it was purposely put here to draw that beast."

Before Frank could question further, the cowboy who went for Doña Matilde entered the room and closed the door behind him. "Mr. Simmons says if you'll throw that critter out the window he'll take care of hauling it off."

"Could you lend us a hand young man? What is your name?" Henson asked.

"Jack Hanks, sir." He shook Henson's hand, and then Frank's. "Happy to help."

Frank hadn't noticed how tall the young man was sitting at the table. He towered over both Frank and Henson. His pale blue eyes squinted in consternation.

"If you don't mind, before we do that bit of a job, I want to tell you something." Jack crossed his arms and leaned against the door. He lowered his voice. "As shameful as it was for me to sit in this bar all day on my day off, I believe I overheard something that might be of use to you. Rather, to Mrs. Riggs. She's been very kind to me, and I believe an injustice has been done her."

Ire rose on Frank's neck. "What?"

"Well, I overheard the barkeep, that Mr. Simmons, hire a trapper to catch and cage a coyote for him. Told him to deliver it to the back of the bar. He told him to set the cage against the wall outside, under that there window."

Realization broke over Frank like a violent waterfall.

Henson's face went red and his lips straightened into a firm line.

"I mean it could have been an accident if the animal got loose on its own, but after Mrs. Riggs entered the death room, Mr. Simmons disappeared for a short time. He returned in quite the jovial mood." Jack shrugged his shoulders.

Henson showed him the piece of meat under the corpse's head.

"Hmm, well, there you go. Here, let's get this stinking thing out of here." Jack squatted and began to shove the sheet underneath the animal.

Henson joined him. "Come on, Frank, help us. We'll deal with Charlie later."

Frank's chest quaked with anger. *"I'll kill him!"* He got on his knees and helped the men drag the animal toward the window. They moved the long table away and then hoisted the animal over the ledge using the sheet. Blood smeared the wall.

"Since this is Charlie's creature, we'll let him worry about the mess. Jack, will you go with us to see

Sheriff Comhars about this?" Henson brushed at his pants with his handkerchief.

"Sure," Jack said. "I don't cotton to that kind of mischief. Do you think he meant to murder her? I've heard she carries a pistol in her apron pocket. Maybe he counted on her shooting the animal or just wanted to scare her. Still, it was wrong."

Frank could barely speak, the anger filling his throat with sand. "I'll meet you there, I have to do something first." He stormed out of the room.

"Frank!" Henson yelled.

Frank's anger made stars shoot through his vision. He could barely see as he tore down the hall from the back room to the saloon. He crashed into the bar, gripped it with both hands, and then dropped his head. He stood that way for a few seconds, and then shook the fog from his head. *Where is he?* He pushed away from the bar and stepped toward the back door, thwacked it open with his boot and rushed outside.

Charlie was dumping a wash bucket in the ditch that ran behind the saloon.

Within seconds Frank had Charlie by the neck of his shirt, swung him around, doubled his fist and met his jaw with force that turned Charlie completely around. He landed in the dirt.

"What the–?" Charlie began.

Frank yanked him up,pushed him toward the back of the saloon, and slammed him up against the wall. "I'll kill you for letting that coyote loose on her." Frank grasped Charlie's shirt with both hands and knocked him against the wall again.

"I did no such thing. I was paid to have a coyote caught for one of the cowboys. He claimed he could tame one in a bet. Sure he was drunk, but I wasn't passing up the chance to make money. I'm splitting it with the tracker. Now get your hands off me."

Henson, Jack, and the sheriff came out the back door. Henson pulled Frank off of Charlie and shoved him toward Sheriff Comhars. "This is best handled by the law, Frank. Go on over to your room and cool off."

"I didn't do nothin', Sheriff. It ain't my fault that critter got loose," Charlie complained as the sheriff yanked him toward the door.

"He tried to kill her, I just know it," Frank said. He swiped his arm across his mouth. Mrs. Riggs was the only person who'd ever cared about him except his mama when he was little, and Sissy. His hatred of Charlie rose to the same level as that of Barney Riggs.

"Likely, but as I said, it's best handled by the law. Now, go on over to the hotel and check on Mrs. Riggs. I've got to round up that tracker, and the so-called buyer of the coyote. We'll get to the bottom of this."

Frank nodded at Henson and then started the walk back to the hotel, but first he had to wade through a pile of onlookers who'd crowded around the door to watch. He heard, "Simmons had it coming," and "Charlie won't let that go by without retaliation," and "Who is that Hankins kid, anyway?"

Something about hearing his name made him remember why he came to Fort Stockton in the first place. His ma's revenge. But he could never do it. It wasn't Mrs. Riggs's fault, nor any one of her children or friends. He stopped in the middle of the street and looked up at the hotel. His love for it rose in his throat, along with bile, because he realized it could never be his home. The only thing to do was leave. But where? Home? Face Ma without exacting her revenge? Take off to places unknown? A strange sensation entered his heart. *God, if You're really there, show me what to do.* One thing was certain. He wouldn't spoil her Christmas, but the very next chance he got, he would tell Mrs. Riggs the truth.

CHAPTER 21

Frank came out on the veranda early Christmas Eve morning to find Annie enjoying her coffee. "Where do you get your Christmas trees from, Mrs. Riggs?" Frank asked.

"We do have to be creative out here. We don't like to cut down what trees we do have. I usually use a juniper bush, which grows in a cone and works fine for a nice small tree." Annie set her cup down on the porch. "I have a different idea for this year, though. People will think I'm crazy." *As if they don't already.*

"And what crazy idea might that be?" He leaned against the pole at the top of the stairs.

"Well, one night I took a walk at the back of the property and the wind blew several tumbleweeds across my path. I watched them blow up the hill and when they stopped the night sky against them made the stars seem to sit right on their branches. I kind of thought of finding some big ones and decorating them." She peered up at Frank to see if he thought it was a crazy idea.

He smiled. "I bet I can find some big ones for you, Mrs. Riggs. I think that's a fine idea."

Excitement rose in her at the prospect of festive tumbleweeds adorning the hotel. But why wouldn't

Frank call her Annie? She thought to mention it one more time. "You know, you can call me Annie, if you like."

He cleared his throat, and a wrinkle appeared on his forehead. He tipped his hat with a "Thank you, ma'am," and bounded down the steps.

Annie breathed a sigh of relief. Frank had behaved so strangely the night of her birthday party at the Stockton. He'd left the table and she didn't see him until late the next afternoon. He wouldn't make eye contact with her and when he did, his eyes were red. Perhaps he missed his family. Christmas was fast approaching and maybe he was just homesick. Why didn't he go home, or on to his Aunt Phoebe's as he'd initially claimed?

Annie was still on the veranda when Frank drove up in the buckboard. He'd filled it with six large tumbleweeds and two large juniper bushes.

Callie walked around the hotel and actually stifled a laugh at the bushes.

The mirth on her face was enough to motivate Annie to keep going.

Callie and Frank helped her arrange the largest tumbleweed on the bottom and the smallest on the top. Annie retrieved her decorations from storage, and they tied the silver bells, red ribbons, and paper heart garland onto the tumbleweed tree. Satisfied with the results, she decided not to attach the Christmas candles, as she didn't want the tumbleweeds, nor the hotel, to go up in flames. She did light candles all over the room, at a good distance away from their creation.

As the guests came in at night, they gave a smile and a nod. Some even examined it, and gave their puzzled, surprised approval. West Texans were nothing if not resourceful. The guests were rewarded for their kind comments with cookies and coffee.

The children came in from Mass, and then decorated the juniper bushes Frank had set up in the foyer. They were delighted and their eyes shone with excitement as they adorned the tree with their handmade ornaments.

Callie brought Hezzie in and they gave him some paper stars to put on the "tree."

"We better go, Miss Callie. The sooner we go to bed, the sooner Santee come," Hezzie said. He took her by the hand and they left.

Annie's heart swelled with joy at the site of Callie's smile. She'd said goodbye to Lem that morning. Lem agreed to accompany Mr. Callaghan's body as far as he could, before the stage branched off toward Atlanta. Annie thought Callie's last connection to Lucius might get her down, but Hezzie had seemed to fill the void.

After the children had cookies and hot milk, Annie sent them to bed. She cherished a moment alone in her rocker. The parlor emanated warmth and festivity. Try as she might, quiet moments always took her back to Barney.

She thought of their last Christmas together. She'd waited all day for his promised Christmas tree, gave up, and sent Junior out to find something. The family decorated the juniper bush he'd found, but their hearts were not in it. Where was Barney? He'd been gone for two days.

He came stumbling in after midnight. "I told you I would bring home something for you to decorate," he yelled. She prayed the children and guests couldn't hear him. She blew out the candles and went to bed, locking the bedroom door. She wasn't about to get into it with him on Christmas Eve.

Christmas morning she expected to find him asleep on the settee, but found him in the kitchen, cracking eggs into the skillet. He looked up and smiled as she came into the kitchen. "Aw, Annie girl, Merry Christmas!" He pulled a small box from his vest pocket and handed it to her.

His brilliant blue eyes, although sleepy and sluggish that morning, never failed to melt her. The lecture she'd fallen asleep planning had dissipated at the sight of his smile. She took the box from him and opened it.

A gold locket slipped into her palm as she took the lid from the box and turned it over. A gasp escaped her lips. Her name was engraved on the shining oval front. She opened the locket and found a tiny picture of herself on one side, and Barney on the other. "Barney, it's beautiful."

He took the locket from her hands and put it around her neck. He closed the clasp, and then kissed her on the back of her neck. "Ordered it on my last trip to Angelo and picked it up yesterday. Took some mighty hard riding to get here in time for Christmas." He wrapped his arms around her.

She pushed back the thought that he'd either stopped at the Gray Mule when he got back, or more likely, drank the whole ride home.

"I do love you, Annie. I know you don't believe it, but I do." He unwrapped his arms and then put his hands on both her shoulders. "I'll quit drinking, Annie. I don't want to lose you."

She believed him, again.

"And here's one more gift," he said. He reached into his pocket and gave her what she always carried in her apron pocket from that day forward.

The children streamed into the kitchen. "Pa!" they exclaimed in unison and rushed them.

Barney picked up Gene, and grabbed Mavis by the hand. Junior and Errol grabbed their father for a hug.

"I saw Santa on my way home, and he asked me to deliver some gifts for you younguns. It's in my saddle bags. Let's go out and get them." They all headed joyfully for the front door. Barney looked back at her and winked.

Annie resisted the temptation to weep over the memory. She reached under the neck of her blouse and pulled out the locket. She opened the oval and gazed at the two pictures, and then reached her hand in her apron pocket and caressed the cold steel.

CHAPTER 22

The front door opened.

"Mija, come quickly," Doña Piña called.

What now? Annie rushed to meet her. "What is it?"

"The Parker woman needs our help," she said. She took Annie's hand and they walked around the veranda toward the courthouse.

The sight reminded Annie of one of Mr. Abadie's films. The sheriff and one of his deputies had Silas Parker in restraints, and Carmelita Parker knelt at their feet, one arm holding her little toddler, and the other grasped around Silas's leg. The desperate wail that came from her throat tore at Annie's heart. The baby screamed.

A crowd gathered. Some pointed, others shook their heads with amused smirks. What had this town come to? Why was no one helping her?

Annie and Doña Piña made their way across the street, and through the crowd. Doña Piña reached for the baby, walked some distance away, and tried to settle him.

Annie knelt beside Carmelita. "Come with me, dear. You can't stop this right now. We can sort it out later," Annie whispered. She put her arms around the distraught young mother and tried to get her to stand.

"No, please, don't take him! What will we do? Please, Sheriff, give him another chance," Carmelita cried.

The Sheriff and his deputy jerked Silas away from his wife's grasp and manhandled him toward the jail across the street. Silas spat at the sheriff in defiance.

"No!" Carmelita screamed and ran after them. Annie caught her and held her fast. "Look, Carmelita, we will go to the hotel. He is just there across the street. You can visit him. It will be all right."

"No," Carmelita cried. "They are taking him to El Paso. He will have to serve a year! I don't know how we will live." Carmelita broke free and darted her head back and forth, as though looking for someone in the crowd. She spotted Phillip Claston, who stood with his wife Laura on his arm. Carmelita ran to him and threw herself at his feet. "Please, Phillip, help me. Can't you do something?" She lay her head on his shiny black oxfords and sobbed.

Claston stepped away from her with disdain on his round, pudgy face. The confusion on Laura's equally chubby face twisted her features. "What is the meaning of that, Phillip?"

Her husband shrugged his shoulders and waved his hand to dismiss the whole idea.

"Do you know her?" Laura asked. She pulled away from his elbow and crossed her arms.

Bessie Munroe, who was standing behind the Clastons, stepped forward, laughing. "Of course you do, Phillip. You're one of our best patrons at the

Comfort Arms." She fisted her hands on her hips and laughed again. She looked around and spoke to the crowd. "He has a particular liking for Carmelita."

"Not true!" exclaimed Claston. "I would never go to that place, or take up with trash like that." He extended his hook nose up in the air.

Annie managed to lift Carmelita off the ground just as Frank, who came out of nowhere, pushed Phillip Claston's chest with both his hands. Then he doubled up his fist and smashed it into the rotund man's astonished face. Phillip landed on the ground, both legs flying into the air.

Laura's face registered shock, but rallied in time to kick her husband in the ribs. She stormed off.

"Frank!" Annie yelled. "What in the name of-" She could not continue for the shock. He breathed hard, and his red face twisted with rage. He leaned over and grasped both knees.

"Come, mija, let's get these poor creatures away from here," Doña Piña called.

One of the sheriff's deputies left the wagon and rushed to where Frank stood. He yanked his arms behind his back and cuffed him, and then started walking him to the jail.

Annie watched this for a few seconds. *Nothing I can do about that just now.* She put her arm around Carmelita, whose uncontrollable sobs could surely be heard all over town, and walked her toward the hotel. She settled Carmelita and the baby into one of the rooms, and then brought her some tea. When she calmed down a bit, Annie left her with an admonition to rest, as the baby had gone to sleep.

Annie joined Doña Piña at the kitchen table. "My goodness, what a morning! That poor child. What will she do? Does she really, um, work at the Comfort Arms?"

"Pobre cosa," Matilda said. "She does, but only when her husband wanted her to. He doesn't like to work, and so he would farm her out. Since the baby came, she wouldn't go, and he resorted to thieving to get his booze. Not to feed them, mind you, but to serve himself."

Annie's eyes grew wide. Had she ever heard Matilda express so much dislike? Well, there was much to dislike. She gave her friend a moment to calm before commenting. "Isn't her father still living? Can't she go to Mateo Riviera?"

"No, he has disowned her. The morning of her wedding, Mateo told her if she went through with it she could never come home. He called Silas many ugly names that meant 'lying, thieving, no account.' He nearly threw his own wife out because Sarai insisted on going to the wedding."

"Oh, my. I hate to think of the Comfort Arms as her only option." Annie stood to make them both some tea.

"I will speak to Mateo. Since Sarai has passed on, he might let his daughter keep house for him. Now, Amiga, what of your young boarder, Frank? He was certainly passionate in his dislike for Señor Claston."

"I can't imagine. Although Phillip certainly deserved it. Surely they won't keep him in jail. I'll go and see him in a bit. Did you know about Phillip's, um, activities?"

"No, I did not. It will bring his service at Mass into question. Well, I must be getting home now, mija. Thank you for your help," Matilde said.

Annie walked her to the door.

Maddie arrived at the same time. "So much excitement in town today. The children watched the whole thing from the school windows. I hate that Gene saw Frank in that state," Maddie said.

Oh, dear. Gene loved Frank so much. Annie sighed. "I feel bad about that. Let's hope he isn't too highly affected. We already have to tear him away from making a hero out of Barney's escapades." She thought of the dime novel incident. "Can you get lunch started? I'd like to go over to see Frank for a minute."

"Certainly, Mama. What made him do that? I didn't think he knew Carmelita, or the Clastons, for that matter." Maddie headed toward the kitchen.

Annie didn't answer. She wondered anew about Frank's history. The crowd had dispersed as she walked across the courtyard toward the jail. What would she say to him?

The deputy met her at the door. "You can't see him just now, Mrs. Riggs. I will have to keep him overnight."

"But, why? I've seen many men in this town go free after a much worse fight than that." Annie stepped beside him into the jail.

"You're right. I only meant to keep him until he cooled off and got a talking to. But you know how the two cells are right next to each other, only separated by bars?"

"Yes." Annie said, and she feared what he would say before he said it.

"Well, Hankins pulled Silas's face to the bars between them by his shirt, and hit him repeatedly. I mean, well, Silas Parker is no good, but I can't be having that. I had to cuff him to the other side of the cell."

"I see." *Merciful heavens. What was wrong with that boy?* "Couldn't I see him anyway? I can calm him down, talk some sense into him."

The deputy cocked his head to the side, considering her. "I don't know, Mrs. Riggs. Both of those men are in bad moods."

"I won't be a minute, I promise. And I'll bring you, and them, some lunch later. It will save you from having to go for it yourself." She smiled, as though he'd surely agree, banking on the reputation of her cooking.

"Well, all right, but just a moment or two, and sit on the bench against the wall. I don't want you standing close to the cells with them both in fighting moods. You know the way upstairs?"

"Unfortunately, yes." She'd visited Barney there many times, after he'd spent a whole day in the saloon. Annie prayed as she took the flight of stairs.

Frank was laying on the cell cot, a flat, uncovered pillow over his face, his wrist handcuffed to the bars. He looked up when she came in. "Mrs. Riggs, you shouldn't be here."

"No, you're right. I shouldn't. What has gotten into you? That Claston character needs his comeuppance, but I'm just surprised it came from you. What came over you?"

He sat up and leaned over his knees. He looked over at Silas Parker who was laying on his own cot, his face to the wall.

"Well, it," he began, and then hung his head. "It reminded me of something, well, someone." He squeezed the fingers of his free hand over his eyes, as thought to stave off tears. He did not look back up, nor say anymore.

Annie waited a few moments. "I see. Well, I'll be back later with some lunch."

Parker stirred at the word "lunch" and turned toward her.

"Yes, for you, too. I'm surprised you haven't asked about your wife," she said. She walked toward the door.

"*Hmphf,*" Silas replied, and turned back to the wall. "If she'd do her work like she's supposed to, I wouldn't have to steal."

Frank stood and headed toward Silas's cell, but was jerked back to the cot by his restraints.

"Frank, it won't do any good. Let it go." Annie said.

Frank punched the wall, but he backed off. He sat on his cot and hung his head. Annie reached the door and looked back at Frank.

He seemed to sense this and looked up. "Mrs. Riggs, I think it's time for me to go home."

CHAPTER 23

The aftermath of Christmas Day had to be cleaned up and hotel guests needed attending to, no matter what had occurred on the town square.

Callie and Hezzie came over early the next day and had already begun to take down the Christmas decorations when Annie came into the parlor to have her coffee.

"You go on and have your coffee in peace, we'll be seein' to this, Mrs. Annie," Callie said, and then gave Hezzie a nod.

Hezzie turned toward her, put his hands behind his back and straightened to his full height. "Thank you very much, Mrs. Riggs, for the new suit of clothes, and for the Christmas meal. Also for the candies and cookies. I'm very grateful."

Callie beamed with pride.

Hezzie's rehearsed gratitude made Annie smile.

"You are quite welcome, young man."

Annie took her coffee and walked around her hotel. She looked out the front door window.

Frank was at the bottom of the stairs, sitting on Biscuit, staring straight in front of him.

She opened the door. "Frank, you were released? Is everything all right?"

He glanced up at her and nodded, but he didn't smile. His saddle bags looked stuffed. "I'm fine, Mrs. Riggs, and I'm real sorry for what happened yesterday. I would understand if you didn't want me to work for you no more."

"Nonsense," she said. *He's leaving.* The realization hurt Annie worse than she thought it would. He had become like a son to her. He was her friend. She wasn't ready. "Will you go to the station and collect the mail?"

He nodded, not looking up at her. He spurred Biscuit toward the road, and then he disappeared.

She'd get to see him one more time when he came back with the mail. Perhaps she could get him to open up about his family. He'd seemed to blossom since he'd been in the community, but he never lost that desperate look of hurt. Everyone would miss him.

She would miss him.

~*~

Frank should have hurried to the freight station. He really wanted to get on his way back to Yuma. Still, he had to face Charlie Simmons, and tell Mrs. Riggs the truth, and if she didn't have him arrested, he'd be on his way. He'd put it off as long as he could. What would he tell his mother? He'd vowed to avenge the family for what Barney Riggs had done.

He gripped the reins until his hands hurt. He'd just spent the best Christmas he'd ever experienced. He'd thought about God without being angry. He'd actually prayed. The time he'd spent with Mrs. Riggs and the people around her had made him a better person. His Ma would never understand. Maybe he wouldn't go home at all. He'd promised Sissy that he would return.

The stationmaster threw down the mail. If it hadn't been on top he'd never have seen it because he wasn't in the habit of looking through Mrs. Riggs's mail. The envelope clearly said Frank Jennings, Riggs Hotel, and Sissy's name was at the top left corner.

He tipped his hat at the stationmaster and then clucked Biscuit to a trot. He'd written Sissy once, early on when his heart was still full of hate. He'd only let her know that he had made it to Fort Stockton, and that he'd secured a job with Mrs. Riggs. Also, that he'd found someone who hated her as much as he did, and they were in cahoots for revenge. He'd written her once more that he'd changed his mind, that he couldn't exact revenge on Mrs. Riggs.

Revenge. How could he have changed so much? If he would be a better man, he'd have to tell Mrs. Riggs the truth. He didn't want to be jailed, or worse, see the disappointment on her face. Then he'd have to face his mother with the news he'd not done anything to avenge her.

A germ of an idea sprang up in his heart. Could he get Ma to move to Fort Stockton? Maybe her bitterness could be assuaged by being around Mrs. Riggs and Fort Stockton. His certainly had. That little hope made him feel better. He almost couldn't wait to get home and broach that idea to his Ma. He'd saved some money while in Fort Stockton, and he'd give that to her upfront, and then convince her to come back with him. Perhaps, if he explained everything to Mrs. Riggs, she'd give Ma a job.

He often pondered how Ma and Mrs. Riggs had turned out so different when they both suffered such great tragedies. Was it family? Was it faith? Maybe if Ma could have read the Bible she brought with her when she married Pa.

He rode Biscuit behind the saloon. He'd read his letter, and then confront Charlie. Then he'd go and speak to Mrs. Riggs, and hopefully, be on his way. His hands trembled as he opened the letter.

Dear Frank,

It's me Sissy. Hoping you will get yerself home soon and glad you haven't got kilt. Your last letter relieved both Mama and me. But I'm afraid I've got some bad news. I'm sorry Frank, but your ma is dead.

Something exploded in Frank's head, and reached down into his heart. He grasped his chest as tears sprang to his eyes. He could barely see to read the rest of the letter. No! He couldn't breathe.

He shoved his foot into the stirrup and swung his other leg around and nearly fell off the horse. Biscuit neighed and nudged him with his nose. Frank stumbled over to the back wall of the saloon and slid down. He tried to breathe, and then shook the stupor from his head. He lifted the letter close to his face.

It was a week ago, Frank. I don't know when you will get this but it happened at Thanksgiving. Mama and me heard a commotion down the street and went to look. There was people gathered around the door of the saloon looking in. We couldn't see in, but we could hear someone hollering for help. Then your mama came flying out the door like she was throwed, and Frank, I'm sorry, but she was badly beaten and bleeding, and most of her clothes torn off. People just stood around and watched but me and mama picked her up and brought her to the laundry. The bank done took your farm, so we kept her. She lived a few days. We couldn't get the doctor to come, but we think she passed away because she had been hit so hard in the head. Her eyes never looked straight again. Mama prayed and prayed, but she died. I know it's going to hurt you, but you have to think of her not suffering no more. We buried her out in the country where some of our family is buried. We was dressing her in one of Mama's dresses, we noticed lots and lots of bruises. I don't know which one of them men beat her, but also none of them helped her. I'm so sorry Frank. Will you please come home? I say "home" cuz your home is with me and mama. I don't care what nobody says. I want to say it again, Frank. Me and Mama are so sorry.

Your friend,

Sissy

Frank tore the letter into less pieces than his rendered heart. A familiar acid found its way into his soul.

CHAPTER 24

Annie heard the sound of boots walking across the dining room floor.

"I thought you left for San Angelo. I have already started a letter I wanted to send you."

"Oh, what's it about?" Frank stood erect, his hat still on top of his head, askew as though he'd been riding hard and hadn't taken the time to secure it.

Was he still worried that she was upset about his having been in jail? Why couldn't he understand? "I don't want you to leave. I want you to stay," she said. "If you have family, maybe they'd like to come here. I have plenty of work for everyone."

He seemed to choke and made a low groan.

"Frank, what's the matter?" She took a step toward him, and he jerked back a step. He reached behind him and pulled a gun from his belt.

"Frank, what are you doing?" She didn't move, but reached a hand out toward him.

"I'm shooting you, Annie Riggs. That's what I came here for." He pointed the gun at her, his hand shaking.

"No, Frank, you're not." She reached her hand into her pocket.

He eyed her apron pocket, and pushed the gun

farther ahead. His gun in his hand shook, and he grasped it with the other to steady it, and then took another step forward.

"Tell me what's wrong." She kept her hand in her pocket, but stepped toward him and placed her other hand on his shoulder.

He closed his eyes, lowered the gun, and leaned his face toward the touch of her hand. "I promised my Ma. Barney killed my Pa, and I aim to get revenge."

Annie thought over the names of all the men Barney had killed. She could remember no Hankins among them. "You may be mistaken, Frank. Barney never killed anyone by the name of Hankins." She lowered her voice. "Let's sit down and talk about this."

"My name isn't Hankins. It's Jennings."

Annie stumbled back. The one with the wife and two children in Yuma. The prison incident. "So, all this friendship was just a ruse?" Her heart broke, but it all made sense. Understanding dawned as her mind raced over his mood swings, feigned affection, and overreacting to certain events. She reached into her pocket.

Frank jerked away and pointed the gun at her again.

The torture on his face turned her focus away from her hurt to his. What he must have lived through as a child!

"I want to show you something, Frank," she said. She took a step toward the sideboard, bent, and opened the bottom drawer. The gun pushed into her back. Her hand shook as she pulled out a little notebook from under a pile of linens, opened it, and turned a few pages. She settled on one page and showed it to him. He snatched the book from her hand and read aloud.

"Elizabeth, Frank, Clyde Jennings. Father John Jennings killed at Yuma prison escape."

He looked at her. "What is this?"

"Read on, Frank." Annie was weak. She stumbled to the dining room table and sat down, her head in her hands.

He read for a few minutes. "These are prayers for Ma and Clyde and me. I…I don't understand."

She raised her head and wiped tears from her eyes. "Although Charlie likes to say that Barney never killed anyone that didn't need killing, I couldn't help but grieve for those left behind. That's all. I just started praying for the remaining families. You're the first one I've actually met." She stood and tried to take the gun from his hand, but he held it tight, although his hand shook.

Frank sighed, and tears welled in his eyes. "We nearly starved. I was left at home to take care of baby Clyde while Mama worked. I wanted to go to school. Mama got a job at the saloon in Yuma, and she not only worked there, but men came to our house sometimes. The preacher took the baby away and I never saw him again. After a while, I did get to go to school for a few weeks."

"A few weeks?"

"Yes, I killed a man that Mama brought home because he hurt her badly. I got off because the sheriff said the man was a wanted criminal, and it was obvious Mama was roughed up. But after that they wouldn't let me back in the school. There was a laundress in town, my only friend, Sissy. She finished teaching me to read, and looked after me some. I got a job on a ranch and put away some money. I vowed to Ma that I'd make Barney Riggs pay for killing my father. He ruined our lives."

"But your father was in prison. I'd say your family was in trouble before your father met Barney. Isn't that why your ma had to work and why you didn't get to go to school?"

"He was a thief, granted, but Mama said they were gonna let him out. That didn't happen thanks to Barney Riggs."

"Frank, your Pa was a murderer. He was serving a life sentence. He would never have gotten out of there. I don't know why your Ma told you that he was getting out. Maybe to keep desperation away, and to give you hope. Maybe she believed it."

"A murderer? Who'd he kill? Are you sure?"

"Hold on a minute." She went to the sideboard and pulled out a box from the bottom of a pile of dishes. She sat back down and opened the box, filed through until she found a newspaper article. She handed it to Frank.

Farmer Turned Thief Kills Elderly Woman in her Bed, Steals her Life Savings.

He read the article, his face turning red. He crumpled the article up in his fist and threw it across the room. He stood, holstered the gun. He paced the room, took off his hat, and then put it on again. He leaned over a dining room chair and began to pant. Sweat beaded out of his skin and his face shone with it. His eyes rolled back in his head.

Annie thought he might pass out. "Frank, sit down." She walked over to him, pulled him back from the chair and helped him sit down in it.

"My whole life is a lie. How do I stop hating a man that probably did us a favor?" He set his hat on the table, and ran his hand through his hair until he reached his neck. He rubbed it as if it was stiff.

Annie got him a glass of water.

"I could use something stronger," he said.

She put her hands on her hips. "So, that was a lie too."

"Yes, and I don't have an aunt in San Angelo," he said. "I've been about to lose my mind trying my best to hate the woman I came here to kill."

"You don't hate me, do you Frank?" Annie sat down beside him and took his hand in hers.

"No, Annie, I love you. Nobody ever treated me like I was somebody. Well, Mama did until she lost her soul to that saloon in Yuma. But I'm sure you'll be hating me, and calling the sheriff on top of it."

"I won't call the sheriff. You didn't know the truth, neither did I. But I think you've found a place here. I think my prayers were answered, in a mysterious kind of way. You have friends here. You can bring your Ma and Clyde to live here in Fort Stockton. She raised his hand to her lips and kissed it. "We can take care of her."

He shook his head. "She's dead, Mrs. Riggs. Beaten to death in that saloon. I just heard today. And I don't know where Clyde is." He laid his head on the dining room table and wept.

Annie sat in silent prayer. Her heart ached for the grief spilling out of this young man. *He's just a boy.*

He looked up a few minutes later. "You don't mean you'd have me after this?"

"I won't be your sweetheart. I am too old for you, and I do not want another husband. And really, you are not in love with me. I think you've just been so starved for love that your acceptance here made you think you were. You and your family are welcome in mine."

"Actually that was a scheme of Charlie Simmons. We were in cahoots together. He wants you dead over some property your husband promised him."

"I see. Well, he'll never get it now," Annie said. She didn't want to get Frank in trouble by telling the sheriff, so she'd just threaten to report Charlie if he refused to stop harassing her.

"Mama loved me, when I was little, I mean. Workin' in that saloon made her a different person. She gave up trying. Why couldn't she have been strong, like you?" He leaned back in the chair.

"I don't have all the answers, but I do know I was raised in a strong family. I know my faith in God has much to do with it. But don't fool yourself. I thought about giving up many times. Seemed like a man got ahead by working, so why couldn't I? Besides, my Pa would have yanked me out by the hair if I'd ever walked into a saloon. I'm sorry your Ma didn't have family around to help."

"If I'd been older, I could have helped. Maybe Clyde wouldn't have had to go with the preacher."

"You have no idea how to find him?" Could she help this poor boy find his brother?

"No idea at all. That preacher never came back to Yuma, and the ones who did come didn't know anything about it. I don't think he'll even remember me and Ma when he gets old enough to go out on his own."

"We'll add this to our prayers. We should talk about plans to have Henson make inquiries. God knows where he is."

Hope swept across Frank's face. "Maybe this is God's way of helping me. All this trouble."

"God's way?" Annie said.

"I listened to that sermon on the phonograph one day. Hatred of preachers made me listen with a critical ear, but somehow what he said about Christ's sacrifice made me feel all warm inside. As though it was meant for me." Frank held his hand to his chest.

"It is, Frank. It was for all of us. I'm glad you believe. You do believe, don't you?"

He coughed, rubbed his eyes, and then opened his mouth to speak, but the sound of someone stomping through the front door distracted them both.

Charlie Simmons stopped at the entrance to the dining room, and pointed a pistol in their direction. "If you're not doing it, Jennings, get out of the way. I've waited long enough." He took two more drunken, stumbling steps toward them.

"Whoa, there, Mr. Simmons. It's not what you think. I've been wrong all along. My Pa was a murderer, and Mrs. Riggs had nothing to do with any of it." He stood and positioned himself between Charlie and Annie.

"I know he was a killer, that's why I thought you could kill this scheming woman who had my best friend shot!"

She'd had just about enough. Annie stood and took a step in front of Frank. "You're drunk, Charlie Simmons. You know that's not true. I would never have done that. There are plenty of witnesses that saw Barney reach. They all thought he was drawing, but he reached for his cane instead. Everyone saw it. That's not what this is really about, is it? You better leave me alone, or I'll tell Sheriff Comhars all about your little plan here."

"You knew my Pa murdered an old woman in her bed? Yet you kept throwing up to me about my poor Ma, and how Barney killed a thief that should have been released and come back to us. You knew he'd never get out. You wanted that land badly enough to urge me to kill?"

"Oh, I can see the almighty, holy Mrs. Riggs has had an effect on you. We both wanted the same thing. You can't deny that."

Frank stumbled back against the table. He bent over and grasped his knees. "He's right. I came here with vengeance in my heart, even if I didn't know the truth," he whispered.

"You didn't know, Frank, and you changed your mind," Annie said.

She walked right up to Charlie. "How'd you think you'd ever get anything from me after I'm dead? I know all about that tract of land Barney promised you. I've just been waiting for you to speak civil, just once, and I would have made the arrangements. After this, you can just kiss that land goodbye. That's one promise to Barney that I won't be keeping. Now get out of here with that gun before I send for the sheriff."

"You haven't heard the last of this," Charlie seethed.

"Oh, yes, I have. You leave me and mine alone, or the sheriff will find out about your conspiring to murder. Now get out!" Annie stomped her foot and pointed toward the door.

Charlie swung around and started to walk out, but suddenly stopped.

Annie reached into her apron pocket and pulled out her Rosary.

Charlie let out a wolfish growl, whipped around and faced Annie. "No woman is gonna cheat me!" He raised his gun and fired.

She closed her eyes against the flash.

Frank leapt in front of her, and then fell in a heap at her feet.

CHAPTER 25

1912

The wagon master's expression as he handed her the package matched the bolt in her heart when she saw it. "I'm very sorry, but it looks as though it was sent to Stockton, California. Probably sat in the post office there for years. Don't know how it finally found its way to you."

"Thank you, kindly, Mr. Carson," Annie said, turning quickly to hide the emotion that tightened her chest. A present from a ghost? Annie hurried up the steps to the veranda of her hotel, juggling parcels from one arm to the other. She set the packages, save that one, on the wooden floor next to her rocking chair, grasped her skirts about her and sat down. She placed the book-sized item in her lap and ran her hand over the address.

Barney Riggs
Riggs Ranch
Stockton

What could he have ordered from Sears and Roebuck, and when? The date stamp read, March 15, 1901. Years ago! Just a few weeks before he, no, she couldn't let her mind go there. She hesitated to open it.

Instead, she retrieved his picture from her cotton apron pocket. His smirk of a smile and that jaunty bowler cocked sideways over graying brown hair made her smile. His gray eyes, although a tough squint to feign strength, could never mask his tortured soul. The heartbreak of his youth filled him with demons she could never help him overcome.

Oh, how she'd tried! She'd taken him back countless times after repeated vicious rows, vowing to love the wickedness out of him. Her faith wasn't strong enough for both of them. Her family thought her foolish for her persistence. Perhaps it was futile, but they didn't know him as she did. He was worth saving, even if he couldn't see it himself. Oh, how she'd loved him.

She closed her eyes and let the memories, both good and bad, wash over her. Her hands trembled as she replaced the picture in her pocket and then with gentle care, caressed the arms of her rocking chair, another of Barney's gifts from Sears and Roebuck. She'd clasped her hands in joy as he'd presented it to her. "Made of finest quality golden oak. Hand polished to a high shine, elaborately hand carved back and fancy turned spindles, the latest fancy colored embossed leather seat, well braced and fancy turned arms, and guaranteed to last a lifetime, Annie girl!" He'd memorized the description in the catalogue and relished the reciting of it.

So many days of love and laughter, building and planting, growing a family, and protecting their community. Barney embraced the package deal that came with six extra children, and then four of their own. He'd come from tragedy, violence, and heartache, but in Fort Stockton he was a hero, and deservedly so.

Yet the demons persisted—the wickedness that pulled him down, and ultimately killed him.

Tears welled as she opened the package. She set the brown wrapping paper aside to find a Two-volume set of Catholic prayer Books. She imagined his recitation, "Key of Heaven, Thirty-two months, Epistles and Gospels Separate. Persian, duplex, padded, seal grain panel, smooth border, round corners red and gold edges." He'd had it engraved, "Mrs. Barney Riggs."

Perhaps at the last he'd finally understood where her strength came from; or rather a last ditch effort to win her back? She held the books to her bosom.Yes, he'd always be in her heart, but now she was no longer Mrs. Barney Riggs. Just Annie. She wondered what he'd think of all she'd built for their family, for Fort Stockton. What would he think about the major change happening on this very day?Annie couldn't think of a better birthday present than to witness the first day the Orient train rolled into town. In fact, the feverish excitement caused her own special day to pass unnoticed, but she didn't care. She'd turned fifty-four on Wednesday, but today, Sunday, there'd be enough celebration to make up for many birthdays. In fact, it would be a "birth" day of a different kind. Her children would have access to the outside world, and the world would have access to Fort Stockton. Such a long time coming, and there were days when she never believed it would really happen. The business men could keep her from their planning meetings, but nothing could stop her from meeting the train.

The Fort Stockton Pioneer newspaper listed all the local investors in the railroad effort. Annie shivered with pride. Her name was the only woman's name in a long line of financial supporters. The paper also reported that the train carried a delegation from San Angelo. Every business in town bought ads to announce how they planned to regale the visitors with their fineries.

Annie decided not to take out an ad, even though hers was the only woman's name on the list of investors. She figured that stood out well enough on its own. The townspeople would recommend the Riggs Hotel, and she'd laid in supplies for extra guests.

It did not go unnoticed that all the events had been scheduled at the Stockton Hotel, including a formal ball. Chef Fournier's insufferable airs amused her. For weeks he'd pranced around town, complaining that the available supplies were not good enough. He'd stopped everyone on the street to inform them of the delicacies he'd ordered that would arrive on the train. He'd long ago removed her name from the Stockton's menu under the biscuit listing. It hadn't hurt her. She retained the title of having the best biscuits and peach cobbler in town. The entire community began making its way to the new depot. All the ladies, including herself, donned their finest dresses and hats. All the children, including her own and her grandchildren were dressed as though it were a wedding, or preparation for a family portrait. She'd planned to change into her every day clothes to help out with the barbeque event to be held on the old Fort grounds in the evening. A fine day. She walked down Main Street in what seemed like a parade of some importance, everyone laughing and chatting with excitement.

The members of the brass band were already in place and warming up.

Someone began trying to form everyone into a group so that a photograph could be taken.

Father Decorme strode up beside her. "Thank you for the new dresses for the Hijas of Mary. They look wonderful." He nodded his head to where the the girls stood in their angelic white gowns. "They are going to sing!" The young priest, she always called him, was graying at the temples. His desert parish had not been easy, but his enthusiasm never wavered.

Annie smiled. "And thank you for the lovely Rosary and service for Doña Piña. I don't know what we'll do without her." It had only been a month, and Matilde's death still stung her heart. "Our spiritual mother, and my dearest friend, will be missed."

"Ah, and you will take her place, for all of us, Mrs. Annie." Father Decorme kissed her cheek, and then bounded off to his waiting choir in white.

Annie shook her head. To be called a spiritual mother with the past she had! It took some doing on Father Decorme's part, and a great share of encouragement from Doña Piña, but Annie finally came to realize that her two divorces did not stand in the way of her salvation. She had had to forgive James

Johnson, and Barney Riggs, but mostly had to forgive herself.

Annie's heart pounded with mixed emotions. She searched the crowd for Junior, who'd be leaving with the train that evening bound for St. Mary's College in San Antonio. Oh, how she'd miss him. He'd promised to return with a degree in Business Administration. Somehow, she hoped he'd take his future to bigger and better places. But perhaps future Fort Stockton would be a place where he could succeed. There he was, standing with Liam and Bart Jamison, who were also headed for college. Henson and Hepatica stood behind them. Annie waved.

Henson walked over. "Well, my friend. Here it comes. You never believed it." He tipped his Stetson at her.

"You're right, I never did. So much talk. But, as you say, here it comes. Hepatica looks a little green around the gills." Annie took her handkerchief from her bag and dabbed her neck against the warm day.

"Well, you know, both of the boys leaving." He cleared his throat as though it wasn't easy for him either.

"Now, maybe she'll have time to come for those visits we always planned." Annie glanced sideways at her friend.

He didn't make eye contact, but said, "Of course, yes."

Annie chuckled to herself. Henson may be one of her best friends, but his wife was in the group of Fort Stockton's society that looked down on a twice divorced working woman. Perhaps it was unfair to think that way, because Hepatica was never anything but cordial.

Annie had come to terms with her "reputation" long ago. "You'd better get over there, I think she may faint."

Henson looked over toward his wife, who was fanning herself quite vigorously. He stepped away from Annie. "They may not know it, or ever care, but all this is in no small portion your doing. I'm proud of you, Annie."

She waved him off with a smile, her cheeks flaming.

Annie reached into her bag to feel the letter she'd received a few months ago. Soon, she'd have very important guests in her hotel, folks she hoped would make their home in Fort Stockton.

Callie and Hezzie sidled up beside her. "I'm so anxious to meet them, Mrs. Annie. Do you think they will stay?" Callie slipped her arm into Annie's.

"It's my hope," she said. "Oh, Hezzie, don't you look handsome!"

Hezzie pulled at his tie and collar. "How long will this shindig last?"

"All the livelong day, Hezzie. But you can change before the barbeque this afternoon," Callie said.

A cheer rose from the crowd as the train whistle could be heard. The chug of the wheels sent a shock through Annie. Her head swooned with dizziness and her legs felt hollow, as though they couldn't hold her up. As the train pulled into the station, the crowd's frenzied applause and shouts deafened her.

Callie took her hand. "I told you the train would come, Mrs. Annie, didn't I tell you?"

Annie shook the excitement from her head and squeezed Callie's hand. "Yes, my dear, you certainly did."

"Education comes," Callie said.

"And loved ones go," Annie replied. How silly to feel regret after she'd wanted this so much. But the image of Errol leaving, and others to follow, gripped her soul.

Callie looked at Hezzie with wide eyes, as though it hadn't occurred to her that Hezzie might leave her one day.

The delegation began stepping off the train to more applause. They were gathered with the businessmen for a photo.

Annie didn't notice or care that they didn't call for her to join them, because she saw something more dear. The mis-matched couple stepped off the train, their gazes searching. Annie threw to the wind the dignified greeting she'd planned. "Sissy!" she exclaimed and rushed toward her, grasping both her hands. The two women locked tearful gazes and memories for both of them sprang out.

The young man beside Sissy extended his hand. "Clyde Jenkins, Ma'am,"

"Clyde!" Annie said and embraced him. "I'm so glad you've both came!"

The letter from Sissy had explained that Clyde had come to Yuma looking for his family. The traveling preacher had provided him a good education and on his deathbed told Clyde about his family in Yuma. Sissy further explained to him what happened to his mother, and how Frank had come to Fort Stockton, and made a life there. Annie wondered how much Sissy and Clyde really knew about Frank's initial purpose for coming to Fort Stockton.

She'd hoped that Frank would arrive from El Paso in time to meet the train, Annie smiled with pride at Frank's job. Henson trained him as his law assistant, and had sent him to El Paso to gather information about a case he prepared to represent. Her friend had gone out of his way to provide Frank with the fatherly guidance he'd missed all his life.

"I'd read how Fort Stockton was up and coming, and might be a good place for a lawyer. I thought I'd hang my shingle here," Clyde said. "My brother, Mrs. Riggs? Is he here?"

"He wanted very much to be here, but his job has held him up. Surely he'll return in a few days. He's quite anxious to see you."

"Mr. Clyde wanted me to come and keep house for him, Mrs. Annie. I hated to leave Mama, but she encouraged me to come," Sissy said.

Callie stepped forward. "Pleased to meet you, Sissy. Mrs. Annie has a room all prepared for you at the hotel, but if you decide to stay, I hope you'll share a place with me until Mr. Clyde gets settled. It's been fixed up real nice. And, oh, this is Hezzie."

Hezzie took off his cap and bowed, and then looked at Callie, no doubt hoping he'd done as instructed.

"Well, hello, young man." Sissy extended her elbow, and Hezzie slipped his arm through, and then took Callie's arm. He walked them toward the hotel as they talked up a storm, like old friends. Hezzie looked back at Annie with an exasperated expression. That boy would have two women clucking over him now.

Annie heard horse hooves on the road and saw a cloud of dust down the street. She looked up to see Frank galloping toward them. He jumped off Biscuit, looked at Annie, and then locked his gaze on Clyde. He stood, frozen, eyes blinking back tears.

Clyde stepped forward. He glanced at Annie. She nodded to affirm that, yes, that was his brother. "Frankie," he said, and reached out his hand for a shake.

Frank reciprocated, but then lunged at Clyde, threw his arms around him and the brothers stood there for a long moment in silence.

Sissy glanced back from her walk with Callie. She saw Frank and turned. She walked toward them and stood silently until the two men broke apart.

Frank saw her and took both her hands. "Sissy," he said with a marked tenderness.

Annie decided their letters must have been about much more than bringing Clyde to Fort Stockton. She sighed. That would be a difficult union, even in west Texas, but she'd do all she could to help them.

Clyde stepped back beside Annie. She looked up at the tall young man. "You know, you look just like him." So much so that it took Annie's breath away.

"Sissy told me that my brother came here to do harm to you and your family out of revenge. She said that instead, he'd been changed. That you changed him. I'm anxious to hear about that."

"Well, it wasn't me, exactly, but if you grew up in a preacher's house, likely you know what changed him." She crossed herself.

He smiled. "Yes. I think I do, and that is a comfort, Mrs. Riggs."

"Please, just call me Annie."

A Devotional Moment

Do not take revenge, my dear friends, but leave room for God's wrath, for it is written: "It is mine to avenge; I will repay," says the Lord. ~ Romans 12:19

Christians are aware of God's commands concerning forgiveness...and revenge, but when wrongs are committed against the innocent, we tend to cry out (even if only mentally) for justice and fairness. Too often, those whom we believe should be punished do get away with crimes. Too often, the accused are innocent despite the outcry of those who seek (and sometimes succeed) to destroy them. As Christians, must walk a fine line to be sure that we keep God's principles. God tells us that justice will always be served, either in this life or the next, but as impatient humans, we want it now, even when it might be misplaced.

In **Annie True And Brave**, the protagonist must deal with the wrongdoings of others. The evil can potentially affect everyone she loves in a terrible way. She struggles to separate her family from all of the destruction. As she deals with the trials that affect them she must seek forgiveness despite the villian's need for revenge. As she struggles to keep her family together, she must also work to maintain her job and her faith.

If you've ever been the victim of someone who didn't seem to have to pay for their crime, or you've seen injustice happen in your community, it can be difficult to "let go and let God" rather than seeking revenge yourself. But, ponder this: what if you got your revenge and then found out the person was innocent? How would you feel? (and would you be OK receiving their revenge for the injustice you doled out?) What if you exacted "just punishment" only to find that the person had done even worse, and your punishment seemed light by comparison? We can't always know the full truth of things, but God knows. He knows exactly who did what to whom. He knows the hearts of perpetrators. He knows the suffering of victims. When you step away from your anger and zeal for revenge, God will ensure that victims are comforted and restored; He'll ensure that perpetrators get the perfect balance of justice and mercy. This is best for all. And when you let go of anger and embrace forgiveness, the Lord blesses you with peace and righteousness.

LORD, EVEN WHEN I DON'T FEEL IT, HELP ME TO FORGIVE AND SERVE JUSTICE AS YOU WILL. IN JESUS' NAME, AMEN.

Publisher's Note

This novel, addressed the devastating issue of Domestic Violence. If you are in a domestic violence situation and need help:

- visit thehotline.org,
- call 800-799-7233 or
- text BEGIN at 88788

If you need immediate assistance, call the emergency number in your country. (In the USA and Canada: 911).

Thank you…

for purchasing this Harbourlight title. For other inspirational stories, please visit our on-line bookstore at www.pelicanbookgroup.com.

For questions or more information, contact us at customer@pelicanbookgroup.com.

Harbourlight Books
The Beacon in Christian Fiction™
an imprint of Pelican Book Group
www.pelicanbookgroup.com

Connect with Us
www.facebook.com/Pelicanbookgroup
www.twitter.com/pelicanbookgrp

To receive news and specials, subscribe to our bulletin
http://pelink.us/bulletin

May God's glory shine through
this inspirational work of fiction.

AMDG

You Can Help!

At Pelican Book Group it is our mission to entertain readers with fiction that uplifts the Gospel. It is our privilege to spend time with you awhile as you read our stories.

We believe you can help us to bring Christ into the lives of people across the globe. And you don't have to open your wallet or even leave your house!

Here are 3 simple things you can do to help us bring illuminating fiction™ to people everywhere.

1) If you enjoyed this book, write a positive review. Post it at online retailers and websites where readers gather. And share your review with us at reviews@pelicanbookgroup.com (this does give us permission to reprint your review in whole or in part.)

2) If you enjoyed this book, recommend it to a friend in person, at a book club or on social media.

3) If you have suggestions on how we can improve or expand our selection, let us know. We value your opinion. Use the contact form on our web site or e-mail us at customer@pelicanbookgroup.com

God Can Help!

Are you in need? The Almighty can do great things for you. Holy is His Name! He has mercy in every generation. He can lift up the lowly and accomplish all things. Reach out today.

Do not fear: I am with you; do not be anxious: I am your God. I will strengthen you, I will help you, I will uphold you with my victorious right hand.

~Isaiah 41:10 (NAB)

We pray daily, and we especially pray for everyone connected to Pelican Book Group—that includes you! If you have a specific need, we welcome the opportunity to pray for you. Share your needs or praise reports at http://pelink.us/pray4us

Free eBook Offer

We're looking for booklovers like you to partner with us! Join our team of influencers today and periodically receive free eBooks!

For more information
Visit http://pelicanbookgroup.com/booklovers

How About Free Audiobooks?

We're looking for audiobook lovers, too! Partner with us as an audiobook lover and periodically receive free audiobooks!

For more information
Visit
http://pelicanbookgroup.com/booklovers/freeaudio.html

or e-mail
booklovers@pelicanbookgroup.com